BISON
BOOKS

Other titles by Frank B. Linderman
available in Bison Books Editions

Henry Plummer
A Novel

Indian Old-Man Stories
More Sparks from War Eagle's Lodge-Fire

Indian Why Stories
Sparks from War Eagle's Lodge-Fire

Kootenai Why Stories

Old Man Coyote

Plenty-Coups
Chief of the Crows

Pretty-Shield
Medicine Woman of the Crows

The Montana Stories of Frank B. Linderman

THE AUTHORIZED EDITION

University of Nebraska Press
Lincoln and London

Manufactured in the United States of America

⊗ The paper in this book meets the minimum requirements of American National Standard for Information Sciences—Permanence of Paper for Printed Library Materials, ANSI Z39.48-1984.

First Bison Books printing: 1997

Library of Congress Cataloging-in-Publication Data
Linderman, Frank Bird, 1869–1938.
[On a passing frontier]
The Montana stories of Frank B. Linderman.—Authorized ed.
p. cm.
ISBN 978-0-8032-7970-4 (pbk.: alk. paper)
1. Frontier and pioneer life—Montana—Fiction. I. Title.
PS3523.I535M6 1998 97-17727
813′.52—dc21 CIP

Originally published in 1920 as *On a Passing Frontier: Sketches from the Northwest*. Reprinted from the original edition by Charles Scribner's Sons, New York.

I DEDICATE THESE STORIES
TO THE GOOD TOWN OF MALTA
AND TO THE CAMPS IN THE LITTLE ROCKIES
WHERE THE OLD WEST IS MAKING
ITS LAST STAND

CONTENTS

O, dimming trails of other days,
Your lure, your glamour, and your ways
Will last while those who knew you live,
And, fading, to the past will give,
To guard and to forever hold,
A wealth of stories never told.
The winters pass and take their toll;
Where tramped the bear now crawls the mole,
And grasses, spurning steps so light,
Are blotting you from human sight.
The same winds blow, the seasons change,
But white men's ways are hard and strange;
We tread on ants, and lo! 'tis thus
Eternity will tread on us.

ON A PASSING FRONTIER

IN THE NAME OF FRIENDSHIP

IT was years ago and early on a cold morning in January. Bill Ropes was busy behind the bar in the Silver Dollar polishing whiskey-glasses with a linen cloth. At intervals during the polishing he would hold the glasses between his eyes and the light of young day that came in over the window-curtains at the front of the place. Bill, wholly free from care, was humming "The Cow Boy's Lament," when the door was opened and Bud Tiley came in. The visitor did not offer a greeting, but seated himself in a far corner of the room and bowed his head. His hands were thrust deep into his trousers pockets, and at a glance the accustomed eye of Bill recognized the marks of a past and protracted spree. The clock behind the bar struck eight. Its tone was sepulchral. The man in the chair stirred nervously.

"Mornin', Buddy," said Bill.

"Mornin'," growled Bud.

"Seems like a nice mornin', Buddy. What's wrong? What's botherin'?"

"Lots. A plenty is botherin', an' I'm plumb sick of the game, Bill. I'm goin' to quit it. Jest goin' to natcherly lay 'em down. Ye won't see me buckin' agin this brace-game of life no more after to-day. I'm goin' to blow the top of my head off. Been thinkin' it over, an' I've made up my mind." He had been staring at the floor as he spoke, and concluding, he bent forward and picked up a dime that some careless one had lost the night before; then contemptuously tossed the bit of silver in Bill's direction. "Don't belong to me," he mumbled, "an' I'll never need it."

"Goin' to kill yerself, Bud?" asked Bill,

as he gave a glass a final, extra rub with the cloth.

"Um-hu."

"When?"

"To-day."

"Well, I'll be damned. Have a drink, Bud. Come on."

The melancholy man rose hesitatingly from his chair and slouched up to the bar. Bill set out the bottle and the glasses, and Bud poured himself a liberal portion and drank it with a grimace.

"Boo! boo-ff!"

"That's the best whiskey in this town," said Bill.

"Mebby, but it tastes like hell to me."

"That's funny. Say," and Bill leaned across the bar, "I don't know whether you've ever read the book they call the Bible or not, but I have. I've read it from cover to cover. It's as plain as a dog-town would be on Rockefeller's lawn that if you kill yerself or anybody else, the game is out. There's no harp fer you over there. You're out; see, Bud?—out fer keeps. I hate to think of that. It don't seem right, hardly. But I can fix it. I won't see an old friend shut out, Bud. Not me." He lowered his voice and looked about cautiously. "I've killed quite a few men in my life," he whispered. "One more can't make no difference with me. I wouldn't tell it, but you'll be dead an' can't go peddlin' it on me, see? I want to help you, Bud, an' I'll tell you what I'll do. I'll kill you, myself. I ain't stuck on it, but I'll do anything I can fer a friend."

"Will ye, Bill?"

"Course. Have another little drink. This one will taste better'n the other."

"Well, Buddy," said Bill as he raised his glass, "here's hopin' the job turns out right an' that you git a harp over there."

They drank, and then Bill pulled out a drawer in the back-bar. From it he took an old Colt .45 six-shooter and laid the weapon on the bar before Bud. "Ain't she a daisy?" he asked. "I used to pack that when I was a cow-puncher. That's the old gal that I got my men with, too. An' that's why I keep her here where she's handy."

"Looks all right," murmured Bud. "I don't care what ye use so long as it'll do the job quick an' fer keeps."

Bill stuck the gun in his hip-pocket; and his coat wrinkled badly where it fell over the weapon. Then he put on his hat. "Come on, Bud," he said, "if ye're determined to die. I can't fool around on the job. 'Twon't be long till the rush will be on, and I don't want the place closed."

"Where ye goin'?"

"Well, ye don't think I'm goin' to mess up my own place, do ye? Come on."

Bud fell in meekly behind Bill, who bent his steps to the river. The Missouri was frozen, and Bill tried the ice gingerly before he led the way across; then, gaining the farther shore, entered a deserted cabin.

A half-breed had built it years before and had gone his way. A hole had been cut through the pole-roof to allow a stovepipe to vent itself in the open air, and through the hole the wind was sifting the dry snow that clung to the roof about it.

"Here we are, Buddy. Nice an' quiet, an' no visitors. But there ain't no great hurry now we're here. Set down, Buddy, set down."

Bill seated himself on an empty candle-box under the hole in the roof. Bud settled beside him. They had closed the rickety door, and there were no windows. The day-light that found its way through the stove-pipe hole fell upon the pair like a benediction.

"Bud," said Bill, "I've got to fix this job up so it'll look like suicide. I can't afford to have 'em houndin' me fer murder."

"Shore, shore, Bill. I know. Any way suits me. Do it yer own way."

"Of course God A'mighty will know you didn't have nothin' to do with it, Bud—see?"

"Um-hu."

"Well, let's have one more little drink." And Bill drew a half-pint from his pocket.

Bud took a healthy pull at the flask and passed it back to Bill, who also drank; but not so greedily. Returning the flask to his pocket, Bill produced the six-shooter and laid it in his lap. "I'm gettin' chilly, ain't you, Bud?"

"Um-hu."

"Well, I guess we might's well deal the last card, unless ye've changed yer mind."

"I ain't."

"Git over there agin the wall then—right

over there where the bark is peeled off that log. The light is better there—Turn *a-round!* Ye don't suppose I want to look a man in the eyes when I kill him, do *ye?* Thought ye had better sense."

Meekly Bud turned his face to the logs. "Stretch out yer arms!—That's it, but yer left arm's a foot lower'n yer right. I'd hit you in the guts. Raise it a little, so I can plug yer heart. Higher! Higher yet! There! That's bully. Now, stand perfectly still, Bud. This light ain't none too good. It won't take but a second. This old gun tears awful. A cat could jump through the hole it makes an' never touch meat."

He cocked the six-shooter. Its sharp-clicking lock filled the cabin with sound. In a flash Bud wheeled.

"*Don't* shoot, ye damned fool! I believe ye would of killed me like a dog."

Without a word, Bill led the way back across the Missouri and to the saloon. As they entered, Piano Joe fell in with them. Bill nudged him with his elbow, and, sensing that the saloon man had something of a private nature to impart, Piano Joe followed to the far end of the bar, where he heard the story.

"Joe," said Bill, "you talk about callin' a bluff. Never again for me. I thought I'd have to kill that fool as sure as hell. It looked as though he wasn't goin' to weaken. Let's all have a drink."

Bud joined them, but after drinking whispered:

"Joe, can I speak to ye a minute?"

He led the way to the other end of the bar, and using his hand to keep his voice from reaching Bill, who eyed them suspiciously, he whispered: "That man Ropes is a murderer at heart, Joe. Remember that."

WAS CHET SMALLEY HONEST?

"SPEAKING of honesty," said an architect friend of mine, "I have found that standards differ and that men are honest according to their own ideas as to what constitutes honesty. Perhaps no man has the right to define honesty for another, but—well——

"When I had finished school, I went to Havre, and after spending some time in measuring the town's prospects, I hung out my sign. Then I waited. Weeks went by. I was growing anxious for a commission of some kind, great or small, for not only were my funds running low, but I was becoming stale.

"I was even thinking of moving to a larger, older town one afternoon when a pony stopped in front of my office. A man got down and read my sign. Then he came in. He was a cow-puncher. He had what I have called since then 'the typical cow-face,' and, even as a tenderfoot, I could see that he was a top hand at the game.

"'Howdy,' he said.

"'Very well, I thank you. How are you to-day?'

"'I'm fine. Are you the man that draws pictures an' plans fer buildin's?'

"'Yes, I am an architect. I can make plans for any building you would want,' I told him.

"'Well, I've rode up to see ye. Heared ye was in town. It's this a-way. We're a-goin' to build us a schoolhouse down to Lindale, an' it's goin' to be a reg'lar tepee, too. She's goin' to cost ten thousand dollars.'

"He paused in order to allow the figures to sink in. Then he said:

"'I'm chairman of the board an' what I say goes. How would ye like the job of buildin' that shack, son?'

"'I would be delighted. I think I can give you perfect satisfaction, too,' I told him. 'When do you let the contract?'

"'Right away, but givin' satisfaction ain't enough. What's in it fer me if I let ye go ahead? Satisfaction won't buy whiskey.'

"I thought he was joking, but when I looked at him, I knew that he was in earnest. I had a high regard for my profession. Anger seized me, and I cried: 'Get out! Get out of this office! I am not that kind of an architect. I don't want to talk to you.'

"His eyes expressed surprise. 'Well, well,' he said as he began to roll a cigarette. 'No great harm done to ask ye, is there? Don't git yer tail over the dashboard, son.'

"He lighted his cigarette and went out.

I watched him mount his pony and ride away.

"Not long afterward I heard that the schoolhouse was going to be built in Lindale just as he had told me. I learned, too, that the cow-man's name was Chet Smalley and that he *was* the chairman of the board that had the contract to let. I got busy, and through my own efforts and a little pull I obtained on the side, I got the contract.

"I wasn't at all afraid of Smalley. I had something on him, you see. If he had interfered, I would have shown him up to the other members of the board, but he was pleasant to meet and did not offer an objection of any kind. He never mentioned his visit to my office in Havre throughout my entire stay in Lindale—and I was there for a long time.

"As the schoolhouse was nearing completion, a woman came to see me. She wanted me to build a small cottage for her. I found that I could use some material I had on hand, and after a little figuring, I told her that the house, as she had planned it, would cost her fifteen hundred dollars.

"'All right,' she said, 'but I can pay you only seven hundred dollars now. As soon as my husband's estate is settled, though, I will pay you the rest. If that is satisfactory, you may go ahead.'

"I went to the bank. They said that the woman's finances were all right. So I built the cottage. It was finished almost as soon as the school building. When I turned the cottage over to the woman, we went to the bank together. She drew seven hundred dollars in cash. As the man counted it out, I noticed that the currency had never been in use before. It was fresh, crisp, and new. The bills had never been folded and the banker tucked them into a large manilla envelope. I stuck it into my inside coat pocket and took the train for Havre within ten minutes after we had left the bank.

"You see, I was engaged to be married, and my future wife was expecting me there that afternoon. We were to dine early at a favorite restaurant and then go out for the evening. She met me at the station, and we went directly to the restaurant as we had planned.

"I had drawn some plans for a little house, and I spread them upon the table. My fiancée and I became engrossed in a change she had proposed. It was the kitchen, of course. . . . It generally is the kitchen. . . . And I was making notes that would enable me to alter things to suit her, when the waiter who was serving our table bent over me and whispered:

"'There's a man out there that wants to

see you. He seems in a big hurry. What shall I tell him?'

"'I'll go out and see him,' I said; and I went.

"It was Chet Smalley.

"'What did you want?' I asked, feeling that the man intended to insist upon a commission on the work I had done.

"'Wanted to see ye, private, fer a minute if ye kin git away.'

"'I can't leave,' I told him. 'I have a lady with me. I shall be here an hour, at least.'

"'All right,' he replied. 'I'll meet ye next door in an hour. I got to see ye. Will ye be there?'

"'Yes,' I said, and hated myself for not turning him down then and there.

"He went out, and I went back to my dinner. When we had finished eating, I excused myself and went into the saloon which was next door, and found my man waiting patiently.

"'What is it you want?' I demanded.

"'Well, ye see, I come up from Lindale to lay in some supplies an' I went a little stronger than I thought. I've run out of money. Won't ye let me hev two hundred dollars till I git straightened out?'

"His voice carried an appeal that got me, somehow. Two hundred dollars was a pile of money to me then, and I knew that the man wasn't honest; but I was young, and 'no' was hard to say. I had the seven hundred dollars in my pocket. We had walked back to a card-table. The place was not well lighted, and I drew the envelope from my pocket with a quick look over my shoulder. Smalley saw the new, crisp bills. He, too, looked over his shoulder apprehensively and said in a whisper: 'Say, son, they all know me here. Give me a check, can't ye?

It would be different if I was a plumb stranger.'

"Then I knew what was troubling him. I would carry it on.

"'No,' I said. 'I have no bank account. I can't give you a check. These bills are dry and look fine,' and I rubbed one with a finger and showed him that no color came off.

"'I know,' he whispered. 'But they all know me. Can't ye——'

"'No.'

"'Well, I'm game. Count 'em out.'

"I did. He took the money and went away. I didn't see him for two months.

"One day I went to Lindale for a settlement and I saw Chet. 'When ye're through talkin',' he said, 'I want to see ye a minute. Come over to Lem's place.'

"'All right, I will be over in ten minutes.' I was curious to learn what Chet would say.

"I found him waiting for me. He led me back to a small card-room and shut the door. 'Set down,' he said, and chuckled.

"I sat down, and he produced a roll of tattered bills from his pocket and counted me out two hundred dollars in real, old, and tried money. As he shoved it across to me, he said: 'I'm a liar if those dubs in Havre didn't take that money you give me without battin' an eye. I jest paid 'em, an' they took it like it was all right.'

"I didn't tell him that it *was* all right. Somehow, I couldn't spoil the joke; so I took my two hundred dollars and went back to Havre, squared up.

"My wife and I were married soon after. I had built the little home, too. One night my wife wakened me. 'There's somebody on the porch,' she said.

"'Go to sleep,' I told her. 'There's nobody on the porch. You've been dreaming.'

"'I have not,' she persisted. 'Get up and see who it is.'

"I got up. When I went into the living-room, I pressed the button at the switch for the porch light. I was close to the door. 'Put that light out,' some one said in a cautious voice.

"I put it out, and opened the door.

"In walked the hardest looker I have ever seen. He handed me a note. It read:

DEAR ——

This old timer is in trubbel. His rope was too long an hes bin workin over some brands. rustle him a good hoss sos he kin git acrost the line. Do it quick and oblije

yours

CHET.

"I put the fellow out and told him to shift for himself. When I went upstairs, I told the whole story to my wife. I was worried.

"'When morning comes, *you* take the first

train for Lindale and tell that man Smalley that it *wasn't* counterfeit money, or he'll get us both into jail for something,' she said."

THE MEDICINE KEG

ON a bitter cold night in January, 1879, Joe Bent stood before the fireplace in the trading-post on the old Whoop-up trail, and listened to the whistling of the wind. He was worried, and his eyes were fixed on the cheerful blaze before him as though he expected counsel from its light.

Three hours before sundown thirty lodges of Blackfeet had trailed into the little valley and camped three miles from the post. Joe had watched them coming before a threatening storm. It was even then spitting snow, and the wind was shifting about to the point where the northern blizzards await its call. The coming storm had caused the squaws to hurry the laden ponies over the frozen ground; and for a mile the trail had been crowded with loose ponies, pack-animals, and travois. Joe's practised eyes had formed an estimate of the prime robes the packs might contain. But he was worried.

The Indians had camped in a grove of cottonwoods. Order had come out of the hurrying mass of people and ponies, and now thirty lodges sent their smoke away on the bitter wind.

The day was nearly done when Joe turned back to the post after watching the coming of the Blackfeet. Although he and his partner had obtained the good will of both them and the Crees, he wished that they had not come. For his partner, Pete Lebeau, a Canadian Frenchman, had gone to Fort Benton. They had not expected the Indians until a month later, and so the trip had been agreed to.

The post was small and there was no stockade to protect it from attack. When trading was going on in the little store, which was much like others of its day, one or the other of the partners sat back of a partition of logs in which a narrow loophole had been cut, with a double-barrelled, sawed-off shotgun loaded with buckshot. From this vantage-point the gunman could sweep the room if trouble started, and at the same time protect the goods and the man behind the counter.

Most of the stock of goods was piled neatly along the walls back of the partition. Besides the lawful articles of trade, the room contained a barrel of whiskey which had been raised up well toward the roof, and from which a small pipe led down through the puncheon floor.

On the store side of the partition, and in plain sight of customers, a cut from a fir log served as a resting-place for a half-gallon keg, which was securely fastened to the rustic pedestal. The pedestal itself was made fast to the floor, and none but the partners knew that the pipe from the barrel in the back room turned after passing through the floor and from the under side reached up through the cut of wood that so innocently supported the tiny keg; so that, syphon-like, the barrel continually fed the keg as a fountain fills a cup. The plan was clever. No one suspected that there was more whiskey in the post than was contained in the tiny keg in plain sight on the store side of the partition.

Joe was making ready for trading by moving more of the stock back of the partition and was spreading some bright blankets for display, when Red Wolf and two other Indians opened the door and came in.

Joe invited them to smoke. Then he lighted a candle, for it was growing dark, and filled four quart bottles from the keg in the room. These he presented to the Indians with the request that the fourth bottle be given to the chief and the contents of the others divided among the men of the camp. Then he gave them some tobacco and bade them good-night.

As he closed and barred the door he became troubled, especially over his giving them the liquor, and more than ever did he wish he were not alone. The storm had grown violent, and the night promised to be a hard one for those who were unprepared. After a time, in the firelight, his misgivings faded and he began to smile at the blazing logs and to heed the battle of the elements outside. Snow was sifting through a loophole, and he crossed the room to stop the opening with a rag. Then he returned to the fire. Smilingly he drew forth a blazing brand and lit his pipe.

An hour later he turned in and from his bed watched the flickering shadows dance about the whiskey-keg like drunken demons. The logs in the walls cracked and popped as the frost pierced them to the very heart; and once when the wind was low, he heard a gray wolf howl near the door. When the fire had burned down, Joe pulled the blanket tight about him and turned over to sleep.

In a painted skin lodge three miles away Red Wolf sat near his fire. About him his family slept peacefully, for the creaking of the straining lodge-poles disturbed them not. Snow, driven by the wind, rattled against the great lodge like handfuls of shot against a pine board, but the Indian did not hear, for he was absorbed in other things. Before him, in the firelight, were two camp kettles, one empty and the other full of water. The empty kettle was of the half-gallon variety.

Carefully Red Wolf filled a quart bottle with the water and then poured its contents into the small empty kettle, being extremely careful not to spill a drop. Once more he filled the bottle and again emptied it into the half-gallon kettle, which was now almost full —so full that less than half a bottle of water would have overflowed the vessel. Then he, too, filled his pipe, and in a very thoughtful mood, drew forth a blazing brand from the lodge fire and lit the tobacco and red-willow bark. Many times he had made the experiment, and he was thinking now of the little keg at the trading-post. Yes, two bottles was all the keg should hold; and Red Wolf had seen four quart bottles filled from the keg in ten minutes. Unless he was mistaken, the one at the post was a "medicine keg," a "magical keg," and could never be emptied. But when the morning came, he would find out—he would see. After his pipe was finished, like the trader, Red Wolf slept.

When Joe awoke the wind was still. Down through the adobe chimney the daylight fell upon the dead ashes in the great fireplace, and the ventilators admitted additional proof that the night had passed. He built a fire and while the blaze grew in strength, unbarred and opened wide the door. The snow was drifted about the post, and not far from the door he saw the tracks of the wolf leading away across the drifts. For short spaces the tracks had been obliterated by the wind; then they were visible again.

After breakfast he busied himself by baling some buffalo robes purchased since Lebeau's departure, and had almost completed the task when in the doorway Red Wolf appeared.

"How," greeted the Indian.

"How, how," returned Joe, and Red Wolf entered the place without further ceremony. The Indian squatted before the fireplace, producing his pipe, which he filled and lighted with that ease and grace known only to the original American; and proceeded with true ceremony to enjoy a smoke.

Near the open door a pinto pony stood patiently in the snow, his steam-like breath enveloping him in a mist that blended his form into the snow-drifts and the sparkling, glittering shower of frost crystals that filtered down with the sunbeams.

Joe paid no further attention to his visitor until the latter had finished smoking and from his Hudson Bay capote had drawn forth a quart bottle and pointed to the keg.

"Two robes," said Joe in Blackfoot.

The Indian slipped through the door, returning with the price of the purchase, which he laid on the counter. Then, taking the bottle of whiskey, he rode away through the snow.

Joe had just returned from the room behind the partition when Beaver Tail, a brother of Red Wolf, entered the store. The Indian traded two robes for a quart of whiskey and at once mounted his pony and returned to the camp. Joe took the robes and carried them into the other room. When he came out Standing Bear was in the store. He was a surly fellow, and Joe had never liked him. He was older than Red Wolf and was reputed to be quarrelsome. But he smiled at the trader as he offered two fine robes for a quart from the tiny keg. Then he rode away with the bottle as the others had done.

Joe followed his customer to the door and was watching the pony plough through the snow drifts when he saw another rider coming toward the post from the camp. He was leading a pack-animal. As they passed each other Standing Bear held up the bottle of whiskey, but neither rider halted until the man with the pack-horse paused before the open door of the store. It was Red Wolf, and he was singing merrily as he dismounted.

"How!" greeted Joe.

"How, how," returned the Indian—who entered the store at once. He walked straight to the whiskey-keg and laid his hand upon it. "How much?" he asked.

"Two robes, one bottle," replied Joe.

"No, no," said Red Wolf, tapping the keg anxiously. "How much? Heap Big Medicine. Always stay full. Never get empty. How much?"

Joe saw that trouble was not far off, but he said in Blackfoot: "That is not a Medicine Keg. It *will* get empty. It will *not* stay full. I cannot sell the keg. I have no more whiskey to trade. It is gone now."

Red Wolf was not to be put off. "Heap Big Medicine. How much?"

Joe turned and took a fine red blanket from the shelves and offered it to Red Wolf, who indignantly refused the gift. He slapped the keg angrily. "How much?" he demanded. His eyes were snapping fire.

"The keg is not all mine. Lebeau owns one half. I cannot sell it until he comes back," said Joe. "When he comes I will ask him how much."

"You sell us tobacco when Lebeau is gone," said Red Wolf bitterly. "You sell us the whiskey and blankets when he is away. If Lebeau owns one half of the keg, he must own half of the whiskey and the tobacco and the blankets. How much?"

"I can't sell the keg."

"Ten robes," urged Red Wolf.

"No."

"Twenty robes," pleaded the Indian.

"No."

"Twenty robes, ten horses."

"No."

"*How much?*" Red Wolf was breathing heavily. He advanced a step toward the trader. His eyes glimmered with the light of battle. "*How much?*" he cried as he jerked a knife from his belt.

Joe sprang backward and drew his six-shooter. Red Wolf slashed at him with the knife. Joe bent his body to avoid the flashing blade, and his back touched the logs of the wall. He fired.

Red Wolf fell dead at his feet.

Joe gazed at the form on the floor and, in a daze, saw the powder-smoke float across the room to the fireplace, where it was drawn up and away by the draught of the great chimney. Then rousing himself from his stupor, he shut and barred the door.

The action brought back his wits, and picking up the axe he went into the back room, where with a blow he broke the pipe connection to the whiskey barrel. The fiery liquor spattered about the place. It crept under the partition and down along the hewed poles of the puncheon floor toward the open fire, filling the room with its fumes as it came.

Grabbing a buffalo overcoat, his rifle, and a heavy Hudson Bay blanket, Joe unbarred and opened the door. As it swung with a creak on its wooden hinges, admitting the fresh air, a flash of flame enveloped the room. The whiskey had been ignited. The store was afire.

Joe rushed from the place and mounted Red Wolf's pony, looking for an instant toward the Blackfeet camp. Not an Indian was in sight.

Then he turned the pony toward Fort Benton and rode away.

THE THROW-AWAY DANCE

THE Blackfeet were dancing a Throw-Away Dance. Every warrior must discard some valuable possession—something that would make its loss felt to the owner after it had been thrown away—ere he could enter the dance.

It was in June. The tender grass that covered the plains waved in the gentlest of evening breezes. With it there came to the dance from the banks of the Marias River, that sweetest of perfumes, the breath of wild roses.

The moon was well up in the sky when the fire was kindled in the Blackfeet village. A crier rode out from it to call:

"All who would sacrifice; all who would show that they are free-hearted; all who have horses or robes they would throw away—come from your lodges. Come to the Throw-Away Dance of our people!"

Throughout the village rode the crier, pausing at intervals to give his invitation. There was no variation in the monotonous, chanted message, nor any demonstration on the part of those yet within their lodges. If they heard they gave no sign.

But when, finally, the crier returned to the fire, the drums began their weird, measured beating, and some singers raised their voices in strange song.

Then came the dancers, followed by most of the people in the village. Those who were the onlookers formed a large circle about the fire, and into the centre near the fire stepped several young warriors.

Some of them threw away favorite buffalo horses. Others cast off painted robes upon which much work had been spent. Trinkets of all descriptions that cover savage finery were tossed aside by the owners as they entered the dance, and as each made his sacrifice he spoke to the onlookers, telling of the virtues and blessings the property he was now discarding had brought to him. Often the speaker would enlarge upon the value of the goods or chattels thrown away, and some of the dancers were humorous in their allusions to their discarded property.

Whenever a warrior entered the circle of dancers the drums ceased their cadence, and the singers were silent while the brave made his sacrifice and his speech. Each newcomer aroused the curiosity of the watchers who expectantly awaited the words that described the extent of his voluntary loss.

Then at the conclusion of his speaking the dance would be promptly resumed with the additional performer, anxious to show his talents and grace of movements.

Twenty young men had entered, and twenty sacrifices had been made when, no more offering to join the revel, the dance grew mad and wild. The drums set the time faster and yet faster. Yips and yells rent the night as the performers stepped to the savage music, and bent their forms nearly to the ground in grotesque contortions.

Perspiration stood out on their foreheads and glistened in the firelight on their naked bodies, when suddenly the drums ceased. There was a murmur among the people. "It is the Sleeping Wolf," they whispered.

It was so. Sleeping Wolf, their greatest warrior, the pride of the village, had entered the circle—had come to the dance. What would he throw away? Ah! it would be a real sacrifice that the Sleeping Wolf would make. Listen, he speaks. S-h-h!

"Two snows have passed since we fought our enemy, the Crows. We beat them badly and took many scalps. We also took several women from our enemies, the Crow people. One was very beautiful. She belonged to White Badger. But we gambled for her, and I won her from him. I made her my wife with the others. She is young. She is beautiful. But I throw her away."

There was a stir among the people. A burning log fell from its place in the fire and a fountain of red sparks spread fan-like toward the sky as Sleeping Wolf's eyes swept the circle of onlookers. Pointing his finger at a comely young woman who sat across the fire with a group of her friends, he cried:

"Little Bird! Crow woman! I throw you away! I do not want you longer! Never come to my lodge again! I have spoken."

To-tum, to-tum, to-tum—the dance was instantly resumed, and the light of a wild thing at bay came into the black eyes of

Little Bird. She brushed her face with her hand as if to dispel a bad dream. Then she arose and faced the group of women about her. She was young—the youngest among them—and, scorned by the man who had taken her to wife, she turned to her household companions for pity, for sympathy; but did not find it. The sneer she saw on the lips of Weasel-Woman, the first wife of Sleeping Wolf—the one who sits beside him—maddened her. She turned away from the fire, from the dance; and with her face toward the land of the Crows disappeared into the night.

She heard the drums and the cries of the dancing Blackfeet—the hated Blackfeet, as she sped away under the moon. Wolves, like gray shadows, skulked ahead of her and upon either side. She did not care what might be behind. There was enough, and she despised it—hated it.

The sounds in the village were growing fainter and fainter, but, scorning a backward glance lest the moon believe that a Crow had been humbled by the hated tribe, and mayhap, too, the wolves, Little Bird ran, walked, and ran again until the sun came. Then she hid away in some bushes that grew in a deep coulee not far from the great Missouri.

Hate had spurred her footsteps, and she was impatiently awaiting the coming of another night that she might renew her flight to the land of the Crows, her own people. She would tell them all—tell her brother, Mad Bear—how her husband had scorned her before the hated tribe.

Great fluffy clouds floated over her; and once a swift-fox came very close without suspecting her hiding-place, as, nursing her anger, Little Bird, the Crow woman, wished for the dusk.

When at last the sun had gone and the twilight began to lay its hands upon the world she ventured out. She was without food, and her moccasins were old. They were going fast, but her wound was deep, and she minded neither hunger nor half-naked feet. So, throughout the night she travelled; and sometimes, even after so long a time, her thoughts lashed her into running. When morning broke she was far from the Blackfeet village, but yet farther from the Crows who were near the mouth of Elk River. She dug some roots and ate them. Then she bathed her tired feet in the river before hiding away to rest and wait for another night.

At noon, when the sun was hot, she climbed to the top of a high knoll in the breaks of the Missouri to look about. They might follow her. She would see if they were coming to take her back. She was cautious, and it was long before she raised herself to look backward. No—there was nothing save some herds of buffalo on the plains to westward—not a living, moving thing. She turned her face toward the east. Yes!—there were objects far away. They were not buffalo, but they were so far off that Little Bird could not tell if they lived and moved. She broke a branch from a sage-brush and stuck it into the ground. Then she stretched herself upon the hilltop, and sighting the suspicious objects over the stick, she watched them breathlessly a moment. They were moving! They were horsemen! She watched and waited there in the sunlight until the day was old.

At last she could see them plainly. It was a war-party, and they were Crows. They had turned toward the river at sundown where she knew they would camp for the night. She was not afraid now. She made her way to the bank of the stream, and stumbling in her eagerness, sought the hiding-place of the war-party.

Before dark Little Bird was in the camp. Her brother, Mad Bear, was chief of the braves there. Her revenge was at hand. Breathlessly she told of her life in the Blackfeet village, of her marriage to Sleeping Wolf, of her daily treatment and final disgrace.

"I will go with you, brother," she cried. "Oh, let me go with you, my brother. I will lead you to the village. I, myself, will enter the lodge of Sleeping Wolf, though he bade me never to come there again. Come, let us go now while the night is young, for my heart will be upon the ground until the Sleeping Wolf dies—dies! Come, we can camp when it is morning and find the Blackfeet in the dark of another night."

So they started. And near the end of

another night Little Bird showed them the village.

"Give me your gun, brother. I know where the fine horses are, and I will stampede them all. I will go among them in the dark, and they will stampede easily. Then I will"—her voice trembled with rage—"then I will return. Hold my horse until I come back."

Mad Bear stationed his men to await the stampede of the horses. Little Bird took the gun and the darkness hid her. She crept into the Blackfeet camp. The dogs knew her and did not break the silence. Carefully, lest she startle a horse before her errand was done, she stole to the lodge of Sleeping Wolf. How well she knew it even in the dark of night! She paused to listen at the door. A horse whinnied in the rope corral, and the wind sighed in the tops of the lodge poles.

Little Bird raised the door gently—the door of her rightful home. The deep, measured breathing of those within told of sleep—deep sleep. She entered like a shadow, and crossing the fireplace that marked the centre of the lodge, stood beside his sleeping form.

Pointing the gun at his face she whispered: "Sleeping Wolf, Sleeping Wolf, I have come back. The Crow woman has come to——"

The warrior sat up. There was a blinding flash that lighted the lodge for a second, and the roar of the flintlock started a hundred warriors from their beds. Dogs began to howl, and women wailed in the darkness. Men hurried to the lodge of Sleeping Wolf.

But he was dead, and Little Bird was gone. So, too, were many horses.

JAKE HOOVER'S PIG

"IT'S funny lots of men deny sentiment," said Charley Russel, "but I've found more of it in those that denied it than in others who advertised themselves as suffering with an overburden of that virtue.

"A man don't look for a lot of sentiment in a trapper. I mean when it applies to the life and welfare of wild animals. Sometimes it's there, just the same.

"When I was a kid I threw in with old Jake Hoover. Jake was a trapper—a skin-hunter, and killed deer, elk, and antelope for the market. His cabin was in Pig Eye Basin over in the Judith country, and you could see deer from the door of the shack 'most any day.

"The old man would never kill a deer that stuck about the place, and I've seen the time when there wasn't enough grub in the camp to bait a mousetrap, too, yet Jake would no more think of killing one of the deer that hung around there than he would of taking a shot at me. Squirrels and birds were friends of his at all times, and he often fed them.

"One spring a ranchman traded Jake a small pig for some elk meat, and Jake took the pig to camp. He was little and cute, and a nuisance about the place till Jake finally made a pen for him. Grain was scarce, of course, in those days, and we had to rustle to feed that confounded rooter. But whenever either of us could land on a sack of wheat we got it.

"Eat! well I guess so. And grow! Say! that pig just seemed to swell up over night. He was a great pet. When Jake would go to the pen with food, he'd rub Jake's legs with his head while the old fellow would scratch his back and pet him. Let him out, and he'd trail after Jake all day like a dog. Sometimes we had to ride forty or fifty miles to get grain. And money, well, we didn't have any, but managed to trade meat for wheat when we found it.

"Jake would look at the pig and say: 'Kid, won't he make fine eatin' this fall? He's fat as a fool an' big enough to kill right now, but we'll wait till the cold weather comes, an' then, *Zowie!* we'll bat him with the axe. We'll have grease enough to last us till spring. I'm glad I got him.'

"One day he got out of the pen. We had gone hunting. Of course the cabin door was open, and the pig went inside. We were gone two days. I wish you could have seen that shack when we got back.

She never was very tidy, but the pig had found the flour and the syrup and the dried apples. Jake's best blanket was on the floor, and it had been walloped around in the mess for hours. A million flies had moved in, too, an' every sticky spot on the blanket was black with them. We were within ten feet of the door when *crash!* went the dish-pan.

"That was when Jake cocked his rifle and whispered: 'Bear! Look out, Kid.'

"He slipped up to the door, and I was behind him as he poked the barrel of his Winchester inside. Then he began to swear.

"From the middle of the damnedest wreck you ever saw that fool pig raised his head in welcome. He was a black pig, and flour and syrup had gummed his face until it was white. His eyes were ringed all around an' you'd have sworn he had on a pair of goggles. You know the way the dried apples used to come, in a box?—Well, a round slice with a hole in its centre had stuck fast to his forehead.

"The pig was real glad to see us, an' showed it, but Jake was mad.

"'That settles it. You die. You won't see the leaves turn yeller, either. You'll be bacon, ye— Look at my blanket, Kid.'

"I was dying to laugh, but I was afraid to. Jake might go to war if I did.

"We cleaned out the shack, and that night we got ready for the killing. Jake got up before daylight and built a fire.

"'I'm afraid it's too warm to kill that pig yet, Kid,' he said as I pulled on my boots. 'It's too early in the season, an' we can't afford to lose the meat after all the hell we've had with him. Guess we'll wait a spell. Besides, we've got a little wheat left an' there wouldn't be nothin' to feed it to. You bet I won't never have another.'

"So the pig's time was extended. I felt rather glad, for I sort of liked him, even if he was a nuisance.

"But the wheat disappeared at last, and we had to make another rustle. 'It's the last time,' said Jake. 'I'm plumb sick of the contract, an' as soon's this sack is gone—*Zowie!* we'll bat him. It's comin' to him, ain't it?'

"'Sure is,' I told him.

"The weather was growing sharp when the last of the wheat was dished out. 'In the mornin' we'll kill him,' said Jake. 'I'll feed him to-night an' bust his head in the mornin'.' He sharpened his knives and talked of the feast all the evening, but I didn't like to think of the pig at all.

"Jake turned out early. As soon as he got his boots on he took his knives, an axe, and the camp kettle he had always used to feed the pig, and said: 'Come on, Kid, an' we'll git rid of that dirty skunk before we eat. I jest can't put it off no longer. Wheat's all gone, an' I ain't goin' ridin' like a madman to find feed for a dirty hawg no more.'

"We started for the pig-pen. A pine squirrel ran down a fir tree and came to meet us. Jake kicked at him. 'This place is plumb overrun with damned nuisances,' he said, an' stepped over into the pen.

"The pig was tickled to see him and began rubbing his nose on his legs. 'Get out, damn ye,' he cried. 'Get away from me! This ain't no friendly errand. Here, Kid, smash him while I git some water heatin.'

"'Not by a damn sight,' I said. 'He ain't my pig.'

"'Oh, come on, Kid. He's knowed me ever since he was a little feller. We need the meat, an' the wheat's all gone.'

"'Can't help it,' I said. 'I didn't bring him here, and I won't kill him.'

"Jake leaned the axe against the pen. 'Why, he's nothin' but a hawg, an' a low-down one at that. Look at my blanket.'

"'Can't help it, Jake. I can't kill him, and I won't.'

"He turned back to the cabin. I saw him come out with his Winchester. He climbed up the hill, and I walked away from the pen. A half hour went by before the pig, wondering why he had not been fed, turned around.

"Bang!

"The pet was no more. A bullet had entered his brain. Jake came down the hill, leaned his rifle against a tree, and cut the pig's throat.

"'I don't reckon he saw me er knowed who done it, do you, Kid?' he said in a low voice that shook a trifle."

A GUN TRADE

I PULLED an old ivory-handled six-shooter from its scabbard in Charley Russel's studio one morning. I tried its lock, for I always loved the click of an old-time Colt .45. It wouldn't stand cocked. The "dog" had been worn out.

Charley was busy with a canvas, and as I stuck the gun back into its scabbard I said:

"That gun has seen better days."

"Yep," he replied, squatting in a chair before his easel.

"Did I ever tell you how I came by that gun? No? Well, it was the crookedest deal I ever made. I was pretty much of a kid then. My brother and another fellow were camped in the Basin an' I was wranglin' hosses for the Bear Paw Pool outfit.

"One day I rode over to see my brother, an' hanging from an antelope's horns near the door of the cabin I saw a six-shooter in a brand-new scabbard. The sunlight streamed in through the open door an' fell full on the butt of the gun. All the colors of a fire-opal were holding a carnival on that six-shooter's butt. It was mother-of-pearl. Wow! I was stuck for keeps at its beauty. There was nobody in the shack, and I pulled the gun from the scabbard. It was silver-plated and all chased with leaves and vines in gold. My heart went out to that beautiful gun, an' I fondled it, cocked it, and balanced it, with a longing to own it myself.

"I grew suddenly cunning. I shoved the gun back into its scabbard just as I heard my brother coming around the corner of the shack.

"'How!' he said. 'Where'd you come from?'

"'I just rode over. Been here quite a while, though. Some shack you've got. An' hello! a new gun!' I said.

"'Um-hu,' he answered.

"I examined the gun again, pretending it was a new discovery. 'Some butt on that gun,' I said as carelessly as I could, returning it to its scabbard. 'Where'd you get it?'

"'Sent back to the States for it last month. Hungry?'

"'Yep.'

"'I'll cook something,' he said, an' went out into the other room.

"I followed him.

"'How'll you trade guns?' I asked.

"'What you got?' he said, as he cut a steak from the ham of an antelope and laid it on the table.

"I had just bought a good Colt .45. It was blued and clean as a wolf's tooth, too. I pulled it, and he took it from me.

"'It's brand-new,' I told him, 'and dead centre.'

"He handed it back and cut another steak from the antelope meat. 'Oh, I don't know,' he said, with the air of a father about to give something to his youngest, 'my gun's a heap of trouble. All fancy. An' you're a kid. If you are dead stuck on that gun I'll trade even. I'm polishing and cleaning that weapon from morning till night.'

"'Even!' Say! I changed guns and scabbards so quick I got the new one on my belt wrong side to. My brother put the meat in a frying-pan, and I turned toward the door.

"There was an old tomato can setting about thirty yards from the cabin, and I thought: 'I'll just try my beauty.' I was standing in the doorway when I pulled down on the can.

"Bow!

"If it hadn't been for the top of the door-jamb stopping that gun it would have rared back far enough to split my scalp. Roar! Say! my ears were ringing like church bells in town on Sunday and I'd never touched the scenery, let alone the can.

"I looked at the gun. One side of the shiny cylinder was all smoky. I tried to cock the thing. It was stuck. Then I saw a shaving of lead as thick as a slice of bacon wedged in between the cylinder and the barrel. They wouldn't track—simply didn't line up, and the bullets had to turn a corner to get out. Every bullet that ever left that gun would be a cripple, an' nothing else would be in danger except the man that pulled the trigger. I was stuck good and plenty, but I didn't whisper. I poked the fool thing into the scabbard and went back to where my brother was frying the meat. He was grinning. Maybe he was laughing aloud, but I couldn't hear him—not yet.

"We had dinner, but he didn't mention the trade. Neither did I, but said 'antiose' pretty quick, and drifted.

"In the Gap I saw a rider coming. It was Bill Deaton. I got the sun to cutting capers on that mother-of-pearl before I got close up, and he says, 'Hello, Kid. God! that's some *barker* ye got there. Let's see her.'

"I handed it out.

"'Say! She's fancy. Where'd you get it?'

"I thought if my brother's yarn was strong enough to hook me it might tangle Bill, so I said: 'Oh, sent back to the States for it a month ago.'

"'Pretty as a white-faced heifer,' he said, as he balanced my gun in his hand. 'That butt would make jewelry, wouldn't it, Kid—jewelry for a lady, by God.'

"'Sure would,' I said, but didn't tell him that 'twas all it was good for.

"'How'll ye trade, Kid?'

"'Oh, I don't know. What you got?' I asked, and began to roll a cigarette. I didn't have any meat to cut, so I made a smoke to show I wasn't overly interested.

"'This,' he answered, handing out that gun you were looking at. It was new then, and as good as they made them.

"'Oh, if you're dead stuck on that gun of mine,' I said, 'I'll trade even up. I'm tired of rubbing her up and polishing her.' That was, as near as I could remember, what my brother had said while he cut the meat.

"He snapped at the proposition as a trout grabs a fly. I rode on, and I didn't ride slow either. I was afraid Bill might change his mind. I'd drifted down into a coulee when I heard *Bow!* Bill was trying his new gun. I used my spurs, and that cayuse was just touching the landscape in spots when I got into camp.

"I didn't see Bill till the fall roundup. He'd been in camp a week, but he had never mentioned the trade. Neither had I. One night around the fire my curiosity got the upper hand and I asked: 'What did you ever do with that gun I traded you, Bill?'

"'Just what you did, you crook,' he said, as he tossed his cigarette into the fire—'jest what you did; an' I'm hidin' out ever since.'

"'Ever shoot it?' I asked.

"'Once,' he said, 'jest once. She knocked both me an' the pony down. That gun must have come as a prize with bakin' sody.'"

THE WHISKEY PEDDLER

TWO horsemen met just over the Canadian line north of Cutbank, Montana, in May, 1886. One of them wore the uniform of an officer in the Northwest Mounted Police. The other was a plainsman from this side.

"I'll tell ye what I'll do, Cap. I'll cut it up with ye. Leave the trail open, an' every time I git through with a pack I'll divide. I'll be on the square with ye, an' all I ask is that ye leave that there trail open; my trail, I mean. I'll take my chances with the rest of the police in other places. You can give me the word any time, an' we'll quit. Then, agin, if anything turns up that means trouble, jest give me a hunch, an' I'll git—understand?"

It was the plainsman speaking. His name was Jim Dodds. He extended his hand to the man in uniform. "Is it a go?" he asked.

The officer looked warily about. "You will never use my name? No matter what may happen?"

"Never! They kin skin me alive an' I'll never squawk, Cap—never. I'll call on ye every time on my way out an' divide even up. I ain't got no pardner. I'm dealin' this game alone."

"Very good, then. There's my hand on it," said the officer. Then they parted, riding in opposite directions.

Whiskey was being smuggled into the Northwest Territory by men who had been buffalo hunters or trappers on the Montana plains, and the game, spiced by danger as it was, beckoned the most reckless among them.

Jim Dodds had been a keen hunter. But the buffalo herds had dwindled, and he was quick to adopt this new and exciting way of earning a livelihood. The country was wild and unsettled. There were cow ranches, but always long distances apart; and cow men cared nothing for what was "none of their business." So Jim crossed and recrossed the Canadian line five times without meeting obstacles.

Each time he called to pay his respects and to "report" to the officer on his way back to Montana. But there are wheels within wheels. Somebody had grown suspicious of Jim's comings and goings. The innocent one communicated his surmises to the officer, never suspecting that there was an understanding between him and the suspected Jim.

"Very good," he told the suspicious one, "very good. I shall arrest him the next time he calls or—make him explain his visits."

The winter had come and with it the bitter cold of the northwest plains. But weather did not deter Jim from plying his trade. He set out for the Canadian line with a pack-horse loaded down with kegs, well hidden beneath blankets and pack mantle. He had never been careless. On every trip he had assured himself that there were no Mounted Police at the point where he crossed the line. There were none this time.

Once within Canada Jim felt reasonably safe, for a pack-horse was not a suspicious thing. So he journeyed along the ways of other men, and meeting citizens or police greeted them all alike with a pleasant "howdy." He was happy, and his mood was a pass along every road, for how could such a jolly fellow be bent upon a crooked errand?

When at last he had reached his ready

customer and had disposed of his goods he began the return trip, going by way of the post whereat his silent partner awaited him. Jim was happy with the thought of the division of spoils. "It'll shore surprise him this time. That was *some* load, that one." And he chuckled. He had sold the pack-horse with the whiskey. It saved explanations, and, besides, he could travel faster.

The snow was not more than three inches deep over the frozen ground, but the thermometer stood at twenty degrees below zero when he rode into the post of the Mounted Police. The officer, himself, was standing in the door of his quarters as Jim rode up. He had seen him coming. A half dozen of his command had seen the horseman also, and were waiting for him.

"Hello, Cap," greeted Jim. "Some cold to-day, ain't it?" He prepared to dismount, but the officer said:

"I'll have to arrest you, Jim."

The plainsman straightened in his saddle. One look at the man and Jim knew that something was wrong. It was the "hunch" he had asked for in case of trouble.

Instantly his spurs were against the sides of his horse, and the animal dashed away.

"Halt! Halt!" Bang!

Jim fell from his saddle. The officer had shot him.

They carried him to a cot in the hospital on the second floor of a log building, and there they laid him down, conscious, but badly wounded. The .45 calibre bullet had gone through the cantle of his saddle and then through his hip, carrying a bit of leather with it. The shock of the bullet had brought a numbness that was merciful, for the surgeon was twenty miles away. The room began to sway dizzily, and then—but he shut his eyes tight and gritted his teeth.

There was no one in the room. He tried to think.

What did they know? What would they do to him now? How could they have found him out unless—yes, his friend must have weakened, must have given him up. "If he has," he sighed, "it's Stony Mountain for me." The thought made him open his eyes.

The daylight was fading. The yellow sunlight came through the wide window—a sliding window—and fell upon the hewn log wall. The fire in the stove at the far end of the room crackled into life. Then a horse whinnied outside under the wide window. Jim knew that whinny! He crept from his cot and dragged himself to the casing. He raised himself painfully to look out. Some one was talking in the room below.

"Well, we have him safe enough," a voice

said. "He will go to Stony Mountain if he lives."

It was the voice of his friend, and hate surged through him as he listened. He shoved the window cautiously aside. A long, peeled pole was leaning against the building. He whistled, and a horse came around the corner of the hospital. It was Bits, his own wonderful horse.

Jim crawled through the window and slid down the pole to the ground. Somehow he managed to mount the horse. He had no saddle nor bridle nor rope, but twisting his fingers into Bits' mane, Jim Dodds rode away—up the St. Mary's River in the dead of winter, wounded, as I have told you, and on a naked horse.

THE POST-OFFICE AT WOLFTAIL

THE stage stopped at a cow ranch far from other human habitation. The driver, after spending some time in pawing over the contents of the front boot, threw an apparently empty mail-sack to the ground before the cabin. Then, gathering up the reins, he expectorated violently, for he was chewing tobacco.

"Wolftail! pardner. Here's where you git off," he called, leaning slightly from his high perch on the Concord coach.

A young man got out. He carried a suit-case, and his tan buttoned shoes and derby hat fairly screamed "tenderfoot" to the silence about him—for the coach had gone its way in a cloud of dust.

The sun was high and hot. The desert-like plains had been baked until they had cracked. The range was drying up. The water-holes were empty now, and as far as the stranger could see there was not a single living thing in sight.

He knocked on the door. There was no answer. Then he tried the knob, and the door opened, for it was unlocked. The coolness of the cabin invited him, and he entered with an air of proprietorship. "Whew!" he said, and setting down his suit-case, he mopped his face with a linen handkerchief.

It *was* cool in the cabin, for the thick dirt roof was a warrant against the sun. A lone bald-faced hornet, worn out and battered, was crawling laboriously up a grimy window-pane, only to fall back and begin the ascent again.

Besides the stranger, a cat had availed herself of the cabin's shelter, and being awakened, stretched herself listlessly, and then, noting something disappointing about the visitor, crawled away under the bunk in the corner, where from the darkness she gazed at the disturber, her eyes glistening green displeasure.

"Kitty, kitty, kitty," called our friend, invitingly. But the cat would have none of him. So he looked about.

"Guns, guns, guns," he murmured as he surveyed the rack upon which hung an assortment of rifles. There was a colored likeness of Abraham Lincoln and another of Washington at Monmouth. Besides, there was a calendar, and a soap-box that had been nailed to the cabin wall. These furnished the decorations—all of them. The owner's brand had been liberally burned on the door; but this had been done on the outside, so the marks could hardly be included in the decorations within.

The stranger finally sat down and lit a cigarette. "I'll have something to say to Mr. Man when he returns," he mused. "Nice, isn't it? Oh, very nice, indeed, but he will find that I——"

His musing was suddenly interrupted. A cayuse had stopped at the open door, and the roll of the bit in the horse's mouth was an unfamiliar sound to our friend. He watched a man dismount and stoop to pick up the mail-sack, drawing it toward him, while the cayuse backed away with a frightened snort. "Strange," he thought, when the horse, trailing his loose bridle-reins, stopped as he felt their trifling weight.

The rider began to whistle absently as he entered the cabin with the mail-sack. He crossed the floor to the table near the window, secured a key, and unlocked the sack. Then he emptied its contents carelessly upon the table. There were five letters and two wrapped papers. One of the papers, bounding about among the dishes there, upset the sugar-bowl before it landed on the floor. The man swore under his breath. Then he scooped the sugar into a pile with his hand and, holding the sugar-bowl near the edge of the table, scraped the spilled sweetness back into its rightful place. This done, he stooped to recover the refractory paper and saw the visitor.

"Howdy, stranger," he greeted.

"How are you, sir? Are you the postmaster?"

"Hell, no. I live down on the river. Circle-dot's my iron. I was just lookin' to see if there was anything fer me, but there ain't." He gathered up the letters and papers, and crossing the room to the soap-box, he laid them in it. Then he took up a dozen or more letters that had been in the box and ran them through, slowly, making sure of every name upon the much-handled envelopes.

Selecting three or four letters and a paper, he tucked them into his pocket. "I see there's mail for some of the SY outfit, an' I'm ridin' that way so I'll take it along. Say, what's in yer cigarette that makes it stink that a-way?"

"It's a Turkish cigarette, sir."

"Bet it is, all right. Smells like a moccasin afire. *Antiose*."

He rode away. The young man got out a notebook and in it made some entries. "Oh, this will be spicy," he murmured, "and coming in upon him unexpectedly, I'll learn much." Then he selected another cigarette from a golden case and lighted it.

The sun had settled well toward the horizon when another rider came to the cabin. He breezed in good-humoredly, sensing company, no doubt.

"Howdy," he said. "And who might you be, stranger? Hungry?"

"Are you the postmaster?" asked the young man severely, ignoring the polite question.

"Yep."

"Well, sir, I am a United States Inspector of post-offices, and——"

"The hell you be!"

"Yes, sir, and I shall have to report the grossest carelessness on your part to the department. Their——"

"You will!"

The man stuffed the mail-sack into the soap-box and wrenched the box from the wall.

"I'll jest make it worth yer while to add to yer report, son. They ain't never heard from me. Tell 'em I said to go to hell. There's yer damn post-office! Go git it!"

And he threw the box out of the door.

JEW JAKE'S MONTE

THERE are uncounted beauty spots in Montana and among them the Little Rocky Range is not the least. Rising suddenly from the level plain that was the cowman's paradise, the beautiful timbered mountains stretch away for some twenty-five miles, and then—where are they? Gone. Real mountains, too, with deep-cut canyons and tinted cliffs; with snowy peaks in the early fall and gold mines that are within sight of old cow ranches, and even an Indian reservation. In short, the old West is there, all there—or was. And there, too, nature and circumstance have combined to prove that contrast is the best teacher of appreciation; for in no other place are there greater differences in mountains, meadows, or men.

In the Little Rockies are two towns,

Landusky and Zortman. Landusky, even now, is seventy-five miles from a railroad. In the earlier days it was not only a cow-town but, because of the gold mines in the Little Rockies, Landusky was also a mining-camp. This combination of industries, especially because of the country's remoteness, was a bid for the wild in life. The town was named from Old Pike Landusky, an early settler, and Pike was killed by Kid Curry, the notorious outlaw who lived near by at the time. The Kid killed Pike in the latter's saloon, and "thereby hangs a tale"—another tale, altogether.

The old town was tough, but no tougher than Jew Jake who lived in it and ran a saloon. Jake was a cripple. He had been shot in a fight in Great Falls. The bullet smashed his knee, and from that time on Jew Jake stumped about his place of business using a Winchester rifle as a crutch.

Mrs. Jake frequented the place at times. Her makeup was in perfect keeping with her man's position in life, and her affections were shared between Jake and her dog. The dog was an undershot Boston terrier with a cigarette voice and ears like tablespoons. His tail was abbreviated and bent, with a withering twist at the end, which was but three inches from where it began to be a tail.

Besides the Mrs. and the dog, there was a horse that belonged to Jew Jake's band of pets, and Jake loved the horse as much as the Mrs. loved the terrier. Some were unkind enough to say that he thought more of Monte than he did of Blanche, and Blanche was the Mrs., at that. Anyhow, no one ever stole Blanche, but one night a man stole Monte; and Jew Jake went to war.

Monte was a strawberry roan, high-strung, and a regular "town horse." He had been stolen from the Flathead Indians, and Jake had won him at the poker table from a cow-puncher of well-known "rustling" proclivities. Jake had taught him tricks, and he was as cunning as a faro-dealer. He was the best "rope horse" in that section, and his rider always got the money in a roping and tying contest.

But Monte was gone. It was Mrs. Jake who made the discovery and brought the news to the saloon where Jake was dealing bank.

Jew Jake laid his cards upon the table. His eyes took on the light of murder as they swept those about it. "I want that hoss back," he said in a low voice. "The game's out. Cash in."

He had caught no guilty glance among the men there, but he would take steps to make it hard for the thief to get away.

"Bill, go down to the agency and tell the

breeds and Injins to watch fer Monte. Tell the Circle C outfit, too. An', Tom, let me have yer hoss a spell. Dick, tend bar."

Then he stumped out of the place and mounted a pony, riding not toward the plain, but up the gulch.

"He's playin' a hunch," said Pete Sharp. "I don't savvy how any man expects to git away with a hoss as well known in these parts as Monte is."

For two hours Jew Jake followed the trail that led back into the mountains. Then he turned in an easterly direction, picking his way over the rough country until he had gained a high ridge that commanded a view of some open places below. Here he got down from his horse and, hopping on one foot in order to keep his Winchester's muzzle out of the dirt, he selected an advantageous spot and lay down.

Below him was a cabin in a little grove of

fir trees, and near by it were two waste-dumps. The dirt in the dumps had been hoisted from two shallow shafts that had been sunk on a wildcat vein by Tom Baker, years before. At times the cabin had been the hangout of shady characters, and Jew Jake likely knew who occupied it now.

Not a soul was stirring. No smoke was coming from the chimney; but the man on the hilltop lay motionless—waiting.

It was October, and the days were not long. The sun had gone below the mountain-tops when he heard a horse whinny down near the cabin. Then two men came up the trail. They were talking excitedly. He could tell that from the gestures they made. They stopped near the cabin door and continued their argument. The light was fading rapidly when one of the men went into the cabin. He reappeared immediately, leading a horse. It was Monte. Jake knew him even at that distance and in the dusk. He fired. The man, not the one that led the horse, but the other fellow, fell. Jake tried to get another shot but couldn't. He hopped to where he had left his saddle-horse, but he was gone.

In a few minutes more it was dark, and he was afoot. The horse might have been gone for hours, but he had been so intent in watching the cabin that he had not heard him move. Not being able to see to shoot in the darkness, he turned his Winchester to its commoner use as a crutch and stumped down the mountain. It was daylight when he got back to Landusky.

At noon he went again to the scene of the shooting, this time with several men. There was not a sign of the horse. The men had gone, of course, but there was blood on the spot where Jake had said the man fell—not much, but enough to verify his story.

They searched the hills. Men rode over every foot of ground within ten miles of the place, and they were men who could trail a horse, too. But not a track could they find. They examined the dumps near the cabin and peered into the shafts. One shaft had caved and the caving had been recent. This was all they found to pay for their trouble—a newly caved shaft on an abandoned mining claim.

Jake offered a reward for Monte, and every one was on the lookout for him. But five days went by. Then a Frenchman came into Jake's place in Landusky.

"I'm 'unt de deer, me," he said, "back hon de 'ill. Pretty soon hI'm 'ear de magpie. Plantee magpie. hI'm leesen 'ard. I'm say, 'Bar gar! mus' be som-e-ting is dead, mebby. hI'm goin' down dere,' an' me, hI'm findin' in' dis wan piece 'orse 'ide. Wat you tink dat, hey?" The man produced a willow hoop inside of which he had sewn a patch of roan-colored horsehide with the brand OM upon it.

It was Monte's brand. Jake was frantic.

But where was the horse? "'E's dead, dat Monte 'orse. Somebody's keel it Monte. Magpie is fightin' ovair dis wan piece ees skeen," said the Frenchman as he poured himself a drink. "No saree, dere is no 'orse dere. Jist dees wan piece 'ide, de sam' lak hI'm tellin' to you, me."

"I've got it, Jake!" cried the Mrs. "Monte's in that old caved shaft!"

And he was. They'd got scared, you see, and shot the horse. Then they had cut off his brand, rolled him in, and blasted the shaft to cover the carcass. They figured that if the horse were ever found, no one would be able to prove the property without the brand.

AT THE BAR

"WE'LL sing *The Cowboy*," said Shorty. "Now, all together, boys."

"I wash in a pool and wipe on a sack;
I carry my wardrobe all on my back;
For want of an oven I bake in a pot,
And sleep on the ground for want of a cot.

My ceiling's the sky, my floor is the grass,
My music's the lowing of herds as they pass;
My books are the brooks, my sermons the stones,
My parson's a wolf on his pulpit of bones."

"Whoa!" cried the leader. "Whoa!"

The singing ceased. A stranger had entered. He was a bearded man. Slouching up to the bar, he bought himself a drink.

"Well, if that ain't the lowest-down job I ever see a white man do, I'm an Injin. Thought shore he'd treat," said Shorty. in a stage whisper. "Another verse, boys. Here we go!"

"If my chin was hairy, I'd pass for the goat
That bore all the sins of ages remote;
But why they shun the puncher I can't understand,
For each of the patriarchs owned a big brand.
Abraham emigrated in search of a range,
When water got scarce he wanted a change;
Old Isaac owned cattle in charge of Esau,
And Jacob punched cows for his brother-in-law."

"Bully!" cried Shorty. "Bully! Set 'em up, barkeeper, set 'em up. Won't ye hev somethin', stranger? Hev a little somethin' with *us*."

"I'll take a seegar," said the bearded man.

"Shore," said Shorty. "Shore, take what ye want. Yer choice is yer own."

A bob-tailed shepherd dog was at the heels of the stranger. His alert eyes followed every movement of his master and those about him. Timid and unused to the boisterous cow-punchers, he was careful to keep out of everybody's way, and, at the same time, to remain on the ground.

The man lighted the cigar and went out of the place, the dog giving evidence of joy at the move.

"Sheepherder," said Shorty in disgust.

"A gentle *shepherd; real* gentle," supplemented Buck Bowers. "Baa-ba-baa!" he called after the retreating man.

"Should think they'd git lonesome, fellers," said Shorty as he thoughtfully rolled a cigarette.

"Lonesome? No!" said Buck, disgustedly. "They always got a grouch an' a Waterbury watch, an' when they ain't nursin' the one they're windin' the other. Ain't got no time to git lonesome, them fellers."

"Never did see that one before. Must be a new one," said Slim. "Wow! but it's rainin'. Big Alkali'll be up, shore. Let's not ride to-night. Let's stick, an' breeze in the mornin'."

"All right. We'll have another," agreed the Kid. And the night wore away. One by one the crowd had melted.

Buck, who had been the first to go, was the first to come back to the saloon at daylight. Ott Canaday was tending bar.

"Have a mornin's mornin', Buck?" asked Ott.

"Shore. Say, somebody's stole my saddle-blanket, an' it's a Navajo, too."

"Where did ye leave it, Buck?"

"Down to the stable. Everything's there but the blanket. I wouldn't take a pretty for the blanket neither."

"Mebby the boys hev jobbed ye."

"Mebby, but I don't believe it."

"Any strangers——"

"Say!" interrupted Buck. "I bet that sheepherder took it. Where's Slim?"

"Ain't seen him," said Ott.

"I'll make a roundup right now," said Buck, and he went outside.

Half an hour later seven horsemen rode up to the saloon. Buck had found the boys. He got down and came in.

"Ott," he said, "where's that there sheriff's star ye uster hev—that one from Texas?"

"In my war sack," said Ott. "Why?"

"Git it."

Buck polished the badge of office on his chaps and pinned it to his shirt under his coat.

Then the cavalcade rode out of town, silently for once. A fine, drizzling rain was falling, and the gumbo flats were next to impassable. Long, V-shaped flocks of wild geese were flying northward, and there were great puddles of water before the saloon and about the hitch-rack. Milk River was overflowing its banks, and Big Alkali would swim a horse. Out on the ranges the young grass was short, but vividly green, while the cottonwoods and quaking aspens back of the town were just venturing to put forth a promise of foliage.

"Yahee! Yahee! ay—ay—ay. Yahee!" Bang! Bang!

One lone cow-puncher stood on the railroad's right of way in the rain. He was alternately yelling and shooting at tin cans that littered the ground near by. Save for him, the lone disturber, the town was quiet, as if resigned to any fate.

Cashelhofer's cat crawled from under the porch and began to pick his way gingerly through the mud. He was going to the shed behind the hotel. Suddenly the cat's tail grew to double size, and ignoring the gumbo, he tore away for shelter as the "posse" dashed up before the saloon with the sheepherder, a prisoner.

"Git down," commanded Buck.

The sheepherder obeyed instantly.

"Don't try nothin', pardner," said the sheriff, as the frightened man looked across the muddy road. "I'd as lief kill ye as not. Come on." And he conducted him into the saloon, followed by the faithful "posse."

"Keep yer eyes on him, boys," said Buck. "If he makes a break, plug him. I'll go an' find the judge." He turned toward the door.

"If—supposin'—" said Slim. "'Course I'm only supposin', but suppose he offered to buy a drink, shall we let him?"

Buck pondered. "Oh, if he should want to loosen up——"

"I—I want to," said the prisoner. "I intended to treat." His voice shook. "I was going to ask ye—honest, I was, sheriff."

He drew a worn wallet from his pocket.

The eyes of the "posse" grew large. It

was well filled. The sheepherder selected a bill from the store and laid it on the bar. Ott served the drinks, but offered no change.

"Has he got yer blanket, sheriff?" he asked as he laid the bill in the cash-drawer.

"Did hev, but he ain't now."

"I'm sorry for him, then. The judge is pretty hard on thieves," he said as he mopped the bar with a towel. He was wondering who the judge might be.

But Buck had chosen. "Seen Judge Cosgrove this mornin', Ott?"

"He's over to Hank's playin' pin—er—a piano fer a sick man," he said.

"I'll go git him," said Buck.

"Wait, wait, sheriff. I want to treat the boys agin."

"All right. He might move, but I reckon I kin find him. Shoot!"

The sheepherder laid a silver dollar on the bar.

"Come agin, sport," said Ott. "The crowd has growed some."

It had. The place was filled, for the news had spread. The prisoner produced another bill in lieu of the dollar, and it went the way of the first. He made no comment.

"Did you want to see me, sheriff?" And Harry Cosgrove elbowed his way to the bar.

"Yes, yer honor. I've got a prisoner here. If it's all the same to you an'—an' yer docket won't be upset, I'd like fer ye to hear the case now."

The judge considered a moment. "What's the prisoner charged with?"

"Stealin'," said Buck.

"A thief? Is that possible—well! Who's his attorney?"

"Ain't got none yet, judge. Better appoint a lawyer for him. He's a stranger."

The judge pondered. "See if ye can find

Attorney Barry. I saw him in town. Mr. Colby will prosecute, of course," he said finally.

Slim went to find Bud Barry, and Buck found Colby in the hotel.

The judge shook hands with the attorneys as they came in, and the trial began on the spot.

"Your honor," began Colby, "I shall prove beyond a doubt that the defendant stole, took, and carried away one Navajo saddle-blanket from the stable in Malta last night. I shall prove, also, that the property belongs to Buck—er—Mr. Bowers, the sheriff, an'——"

"May it please yer honor," Barry's voice drowned Colby's. "My client wants to buy a drink for the judge and those here assembled. I move the court that he be permitted to do so."

"The court will entertain the motion,"

said Cosgrove. "Court is recessed for five minutes."

At the expiration of the allotted time the judge rapped upon the card-table. Order was promptly resumed.

"Proceed, Mr. Colby," said the court.

"I shall also prove," continued Colby, "that the prisoner at the bar—the bar of justice, yer honor—is a dissolute character, and I will show by my witnesses that other crimes than the one he is now charged with are standing against him in another State. Your honor, murder is——"

"May it please the honorable court," again Bud Barry interrupted, "my client begs, nay, implores, the court to allow him an opportunity to show his respect and esteem for this city by purchasing further refreshments. I therefore move the court, asking the indulgence of the gifted prosecuting attorney, that we recess for five minutes."

"The court stands recessed for five minutes," said the judge.

That round of drinks cost fifteen dollars. The place was packed to the door. The sheepherder's pile dwindled fast.

Wedged between two members of the "posse" Buck found him in the crowd. "I'm sorry for you," he whispered. "I've jest heared the boys talkin'. They want to hang ye. Yer hoss is standin' out in front an' I'm goin' to help ye. I've got back my blanket an' I don't hold no grudge. When the court calls to order I'll start a fight. Listen to me careful."

"I'm listenin'," said the trembling man.

"Well, ye'd better or they'll hang ye. Jest as soon as the judge raps on that table I'll jump onto the prosecutin' attorney. That'll start a row, see? Soon's it starts, you git. Git out of that door an' onto yer hoss. Then ride like hell. Don't stop, an' don't never come back."

"I won't if I can only git away," quavered the man.

Rap, rap, rap. It was the court pounding the table with the butt of a six-shooter. There was instant commotion. The scheduled row was sudden, and Buck's onslaught fierce.

Interest was transferred to the fight, which all but two or three thought was on the square, when a horse tore out of town followed by a dog. The water splashed from the puddles as he passed.

"Pore little dog," said Buck. "It's a gait he ain't never hit before—but he's got a nose, an' he kin trail him, mebby," he laughed. "Set 'em up, Ott."

PAP'S PINTO

"WE were away up on the Madison once, Andy Stevens and I," said Bill. "We'd been hunting elk, and our horses set us afoot. They'd gone, and we spent several days hunting them before we decided they had pulled out for good. It was high time we were getting out, and one night we were discussing ways and means when an old man came into the light of our camp-fire. His hair was white, and he wore a long beard. He was slim and not very tall. His eyes were blue; and his name was Pap Medders. Pap was an old prospector; one of the school that have followed the buffalo to the Sand Hills, you know. He sat down and we told him that we were afoot.

" 'Hosses?' he asked.

" 'Yes, horses,' said Andy.

"Pap poked the fire spitefully. 'Humph,' he said. 'I uster use hosses in these mountains till experience led me agin the fact that God A'mighty wa'n't jokin' when he made a burro. An' he wa'n't. He made him a-purpose. You always know where a burro is at. It don't matter where or when ye camp the first thing ye see when ye poke yer head out of yer blankets in the mornin' is a pair of jackass ears. Ye kin camp in a blizzard or on a desert where there ain't enough grass to chink the cracks between the ribs of a sand-fly. It don't make no difference. Mr. Burro is with ye when ye want to move.

"'On the other hand take a cayuse. Camp on the best spot the Lord ever fertilized fer feed, an' when ye wake up in the mornin' what do ye see? His tracks! Yes, sir, his doggone tracks a-p'intin' out of the country. That's what ye see. Hosses nigh wore me out. I'd git mad an' tie 'em up nights figgerin' I'd sooner see their bones at daybreak than their trail down a gulch. Then I'd git sorry fer 'em tied up at night that way an' turn 'em loose. Shore as I did I'd spend a week lookin' fer 'em.

"'I hed a pack-hoss once—hed several, fer as that's concerned, but the one I want to tell ye of was the one that weaned me fer keeps. He was a glass-eyed, Roman-nosed pinto, with one real soft, bluish eye that looked like it belonged to a choir-singer. The other one was no relation to it, an' the devil peeped from under the lashes that hid it when he slept. I got him from a half-breed on the Flathead Reservation, an' I'm a-bettin' that all the cayuse cussedness that wa'n't bound up in his hide is hid away somewhere in the make-up of a rattlesnake. There couldn't a-been enough left over after his creation to have enthused a much bigger carcass. His end was sudden an' some painful, but when I look back I ain't burdened none with remorse ner regret, fer he courted it from the time I first got my rope on him till he went an' made the play that won him a place in memory.

" ''Twas ten years ago, an' I was on my way to a minin' stampede, south. I hed my twenty-five years' gatherin' on the lump o' cussedness, an' was a-hittin' the trail across the country afoot. Him an' me hed no end o' trouble tryin' to boss the outfit. I uster tie him up o' nights on account of his noticeable desire to quit the game, an' every mornin' I'd hev to break him all over agin. I'd blindfold him, tie up a leg, an' pack him, but ye never could tell when he'd turn himself to buckin' in the middle of the day. I hed many a narrow escape from losin' him an' my outfit, but managed to snub him up by diggin' my heels into the ground an' stayin' with him. Mean! That devil hed even the magpies buffaloed, an' I never knowed one to fly over his shadder fer fear o' bad luck. He was fit fer one thing, an' that was to bait a bear-trap in the foot-hills, somewheres.

"'When that hoss first commenced a real flirtation with fate was one night when I'd camped in a bad stretch o' desert. It got dark on me, an' I hed to hev daylight not knowin' the country, so I found a place where there was jest enough feed to keep the pinto prospectin'. I pulled the pack, looked high an' low fer a picket-pin I'd been packin', but 'twas gone, so I jest held onto the rope an' let him feed around while I ate a bite. There wa'n't nothin' to build a fire out of, an' I could see that a storm was brewin'. It was only April, an' the weather was uncertain. The sky was gittin' black, an' the wind must hev slid over a snowbank some place, fer it felt as chilly as frog legs agin the back o' my neck. It come in gusts. Then it would die down till it sounded like somebody was whisperin' behind me, an' I felt like I'd been doin' somethin' that was drawin' interest.

"'I tied my pet to the pack-saddle, after fixin' it fer a pillow, an' crawled into the blankets, allowin' to keep a hold of the cinch of the saddle in order to be ready to help him finish anything he might start. I'd bought some new woollen drawers. They was coarse an' irritated my skin. I didn't expect to sleep none, but I figgered I'd rest a lot better with them drawers off, so I shed 'em. That's where I was a fool, but I tucked 'em under the blankets with my pants. To make sure of the pinto I spread the pack mantle over the bed and then tied the cinch of the saddle to it. I was dead sure I could ketch hold of it somewhere if he should pull the saddle from under my head.

"'I'd been in bed about an hour when I felt a drop of rain on my face. A few minutes later a big black cloud that had been creepin' up over me began to let out sleet. It wa'n't so bad at first, an' the canvas mantle kept the blankets dry. But the hoss got to snortin' an' pawin' till he made me nervous. Then the wind began to whoop it up, an' at every extra hard gust the pinto would try the rope. It was half sleet and half snow now, an' it cut my face till I could hardly stand it. It was freezin' to the bed an' the camp truck, an' I couldn't see six inches ahead of my nose. I was cussin' myself fer takin' them pants an' drawers off when z-z-zip! went the pack mantle over my head. It was covered with ice an' was stiff as a rawhide. The noise it made scared the pinto, an' in the mix-up I lost my hold on the mantle. My hands was numb. I couldn't hang on, an' away he went, draggin' the pack-saddle, mantle, an' rope into the night.

"'I lit on my feet, runnin' like a wild man —runnin' after a stampeded hoss in a blizzard an' in the dark.

"'When I come to my senses an' tumbled to the fix I was in I stopped an' listened, but the wind sung in my ears an' drowned any sound I might have heard if the night had been still. The stingin' sleet cut my bare legs like the lash of a four-hoss whip. My feet was so numb that I didn't even feel the cactus I stepped on, but I knowed I'd feel 'em next day, if I lived. God! how the wind did blow. It jest seemed that it would lift the boulders out of the ground. I knowed I couldn't foller the pinto, so I started back fer the bed.

"'Then a truth that made my hair white pried itself into my brain. I didn't have no more idea where that bed was than a blind mole. I jest weakened then; an' shivered. I was learnin' a lesson that night that I know by heart till yit.

"'I wandered around. I had to. Every time a big gust would come I'd honker down an' try to shield as much of me as I could. The parts that had to take it felt like they was bleedin'. An' dark! Ye couldn't have drilled a hole in the blackness with a ten-pound hammer an' inch steel. Where there wasn't any cactus there was rocks, an' they was slippery as all time. I'd fall; and it took all my nerve to keep down a sneakin' desire to give it up. But it was a fall that brought me luck. I went kerflop, an' heared a noise near me. I knowed it was the pinto's hoofs agin the rocks. I figgered the saddle had ketched an' hung him up. An' it had.

"'I got him. He tried to bolt, but I hung on like a wood-tick. I couldn't untie the rope from the saddle cinch, so I had to drag the mantle an' pack the saddle. I set the hoss to work by makin' him trot around me, figurin' he'd let me know if he hit the blankets by raisin' hell, an' he did. 'Most got away, but I held on till me an' the saddle hung up in a rock pile not far from the bed. I got back to it, but it was a mass of ice an' partly covered with snow. Daylight was hours off yit, so I wrapped the driest of the blankets around me an' kept the pinto company till daylight. I'd a-killed him if I'd dared, but I was afraid I couldn't pack enough on my back to git me out.

"'The storm let up when mornin' come. Soon's I could see I got the pack onto the pinto, an' pulled out, without eatin' anything, allowin' to make camp at the first wood an' water I run across.

"'Along about noon the sun come out. My clothes was a-warmin' up some. The pack was a-steamin' like wet blankets always do in the sun, an' I was feelin' a little more like myself. I was sufferin' a heap, but awful thankful to git out alive. There was signs o' grass showin' now an' agin, an' I allowed that I was soon goin' to find a place where I could make another camp. The thought of a chance fer coffee was a-makin' my mouth water—when the pinto got a "wire" from the devil an' bolted.

"'I was so doggone sore an' stiff that I wa'n't quick enough to snub him, an' the rope sizzed through my hands like a hot iron. He was gone with my grub an' blankets, an' me God only knowed how fer from a camp or settlement. I started to run after him, knowin' that my life depended on ketchin' him, but he disappeared over a hill with everything lashed to his ornery back. Runnin' was mighty painful to me, but I figgered it was my last sprint, most likely, an' I done the best that was in me. I hiked up the hill he'd gone over, an' when I got to the top I spots him jest makin' the next raise o' ground, about a quarter away, hittin' the high spots in his effort to leave me fer the coyotes.

" 'Soon's I got my eye on him I dropped to one knee, took a rest with my elbow agin the other, drawed a bead on his anatomy with my old Sharps, an' sent a .45 a-whistlin' into his constitution. He went over in a pile, an' I took my own time a-gittin' to him an' unpackin'.

" 'Whenever I hear a feller tellin' what a friend to man a hoss is, me an' memory takes a little sneak back through the years to a pile o' bones on the desert; where in the shadders I kin see the only creature that ever sighed fer the pinto—that creature bein' a buzzard.' "

THE BULLET'S PROOF

BILL DEETS laid a dry stick on the fire and spread his hands before the blaze. "It's a mean cuss that'll shoot a man when his hands are up," he said. "Yet I know a case where it was done; an' the worst of it is the murdered man had been a pardner of the feller that killed him. Put them two facts together an' prove 'em on a man; then if he ain't fit for hell-fire, the devil's been slandered.

"You remember when the Great Northern train was held up years ago near Belton, of course? Well, Jack White, the leader of the gang, got away. He was supposed to have hid in the hills. The railroad company and the Government, an' I reckon the State, too, offered rewards for him, dead or alive, but no one ever found him. It was a big chunk of money that they put up, but I forget just how much it was. Around five thousand dollars, I guess.

"I was camped near the South Fork of the Flathead. 'Twa'n't far from Belton; about three miles, mebby. I'd been there all the summer and fall. The holdup was along in February, near as I remember now. And I was figuring on a move as soon as the break-up came in the spring. One night a man came into camp. I knew him as soon's I set eyes on him. It was Jack White. We'd known each other over on the other side.

"'What you doin' here, man? Don't ye know there's big money up for your scalp?'

"'Yes,' he told me. 'I know they'll pay for me, dead or alive, but I didn't figure you was that kind of a friend, Bill.'

"'I ain't,' I says. 'I don't want no blood-money no time, but I don't want you to hang around here, neither. I want you to drift. I ain't seen you—not yet, anyway.'

"'Bill,' he says, 'I ain't got a cent. I'm clean out of grub and every ca'tridge is gone. Can't ye stake me?'

"'There's some grub there. Steal it,' I says. 'What you shootin'?'

"'Forty-five Colt an' 40–82 Winchester.'

"'I can't do nothin' for you, Jack,' I says, after he told me. 'Might take a blanket. I ain't lookin'. Nights are cold.'

"'I'm in a bad fix, Bill,' he says. 'Won't you go down to the valley an' tell Curley to bring me some ammunition an' some money?'

"'Curley!' I says. 'I wouldn't trust that man farther'n I could see him through my rifle sights.'

"'Mebby not,' he says, 'but Curley is an old pardner of mine. We have set around camp-fires together. Besides that, he owes me a chunk of money—borrowed money.

I'll trust him if you'll go an' tell him where he can find me.'

"I went. Curley said he'd come up the next day. I didn't want to figure in it, so I left camp to hunt deer. White had left it, too, an' had made him a place somewhere close. I didn't know just where, an' I didn't want to know, neither.

"I'll never forget that day. I was touchy as a girl. When I'd step on snow that was crusted the noise my moccasins made would make my back prickle. I couldn't seem to keep my mind off Jack White. I jumped a dozen deer but didn't git a shot. Finally I decided to go back to camp. Something seemed to pull me that way. I hadn't gone far on the back trail when I heard a twig pop. I stopped an' looked careful. Then I saw two men coming up a deer trail. One of 'em was Curley. The other feller was a stranger.

"'Mighty cur'ous route,' I thought, 'if they're on the square.' Pretty soon they saw me, an' Curley got nervous with his Winchester.

"'Where you goin'?' I asked.

"'Goin' to arrest White. Where is he?' he says.

"'How do I know where he is now?' An' I looked him in the eye. I made up my mind pretty quick that I stood to git in bad, so I turned an' tried to hunt agin.

"They went on toward my camp. I felt rotten. I felt worse'n I can tell *ye*; but, you see, if I cut in, I'd be guilty of something er other. So I tried to find a deer. A half hour that seemed lots longer went by. Then I gave it up. I just couldn't hunt.

"I started for camp. *Bang!* I wasn't one hundred yards from the place when I heard a shot. 'Poor old Jack,' I thought. 'They've got ye.'

"They had, too. He was lyin' in the trail when I come up, an' them two was standin' by him. All the mad I own flared up in me.

"'What did you kill him for? Yer own pardner, too, you skunk,' I says to Curley.

"'Well—well,' he stammers. 'I told him to put up his hands, and he wouldn't. He went for his gun. I had to shoot quick. I knew him, an' he was a bad man.'

"'Was he?' I says.

"Then I pulled Jack White's gun from its scabbard an' showed it to 'em. There wasn't a ca'tridge in it.

"After that I leaned over Jack an' tried to stick my finger in the bullet-hole. His arms were down, an' my finger wouldn't go in. I raised his arms up over his head. My finger slipped right into the wound. See?"

THE INDIAN'S GOD

"HIDDEN in most folks, if not in all, there is a sentiment for religion, because all men are naturally religious," said the Major. "You don't believe it? Well, they are, and the tendency has been a curse as well as a blessing, for designing prophets have led them over crooked trails. And yet—well, let me tell you of an old fellow I used to know.

"Uncle Billy we called him then, and Uncle Billy will do now. He was an old prospector and miner who came to Montana in the early sixties. When I knew him he was working a little gold lead in Madison county—the 'Camp-Robber,' he called it. The vein was small, but the 'pay' was gold and it was 'free' in the ore. So the old fellow worked it through an arastra, the crudest, and at the same time the surest way of saving gold yet discovered, I reckon.

"Uncle Billy was a bachelor, of course, and I used to visit him often. He was a keen-minded old man and neat as a pin. He had lived alone most of his life and was somewhat of a crank because he had. Most of them are, you know. But I surprised my friend one Sunday morning.

"I was near to the camp when the great beauty of the day halted me in the little clearing near Uncle Billy's cabin. The sun was rising over the big peak on the far side of the gulch, and his rays, like messengers, sped on down the rough mountain-side to wake the flowers and crawling things and warn them of his coming. A yellowhammer drummed on the dead top of a pine away in the wilds, where, high up in the golden light that glinted on his bright wing-feathers, his call woke the choirs in the thickets below.

And even as the bird-song grew in volume I felt ever more keenly the silence of the great open country.

"Uncle Billy, standing on a mossy mound where the bluebells grew in clusters, was watching the sun rise, and so absorbed was he that for long I did not speak. Erect, with arms folded, bare-headed, and silent, the old man stood until the flood-light fell full upon him; when he murmured 'Amen.'

"I was startled, but he turned slowly, and without showing the least surprise, said: 'Good mornin', friend. Ye're early. Sit down and we'll have a smoke.'

"Without further speech he began cutting tobacco for his pipe, which he filled and lighted. Then as a wreath of the fragrant mist floated past me he said:

"'I had an Injin pardner once, an' after he had gone his way all of a sudden it came to me that he was right in a heap of things.

I used to watch that Injin because he was a good man; and from him I learned some queer things that seemed to fit into my own life—so I adopted 'em.

"'First of all I noticed that every beauty spot in nature was a shrine to him. He didn't tell me so, but I saw it and felt it. Before a brilliant sunset or a noisy waterfall he'd stand in silent admiration; an' I learned, after a while, that in each case he offered up his prayer to The Great Mystery. He had but one prayer, an' he told me that one: Let my children all grow old. That was all, an' it was never varied. It made me ashamed of myself an' my race. Once he told me that the birds were little people, an' after I'd learned to look an' listen, myself, I noticed that they had each just one sure-enough song, an' some of 'em only a single note. Then I thought of his only prayer.

"'I could talk to you for an hour about things I learned from that Injin. But he was an unwilling teacher, because he seemed to think that all live things believe an' think just as he did. Once I asked him: "Who is God?" an' he replied: "The sun, the earth, the flowers, the birds, the big trees, the people, the fire, an' the water is God. Sometimes they speak to me, an' I'm glad in my heart. Big trees speak the loudest to me. Others hear other things best."

"'He seemed surprised at my question—seemed to think I must be jokin' him. But I'm mighty glad he answered as he did, for it blazed a new trail for me. I feel better toward my fellows an' I only pray for peace. It took a long, long time, but now I know

"'"The redman dares an only prayer;
One perfume has the rose;
When mornin' dawns, the robin sings
The only song he knows.

The silent are the giant things
  That make the temple grand
Amid a peace that nature meant
  All men should understand.'' ''

BRAVERY

"I THINK Major Reno was a coward," said Dick Mosby at the conclusion of a discussion of the Custer fight on the Little Big Horn.

"Maybe he was," said the Doctor. "But a man cannot help it if he is born a coward. Men are brave because nature made them to be not afraid. It must be harder to be a coward than to be a brave man, especially among other brave men. And, of course, there are degrees of bravery. Some men are brave to rashness. General Custer was brave. Some say he was rash in his bravery."

"What was the bravest deed you ever witnessed, Doctor?" asked Dick.

"I shall not have to search my memory,"

replied the Doctor. "I have never forgotten. It was on September 13, 1890. Hugh Boyle had been killed by Head Chief and Young Mule, Cheyennes. Trouble had followed the killing, and the Indians had admitted their guilt. They had offered to give up their ponies and all of their worldly goods to square the account, but of course the authorities would not listen. They demanded the surrender of Head Chief and Young Mule. They were to be tried and hanged if found guilty; and as the Indians had freely admitted the killing their execution was a certainty, if they gave themselves up.

"The Cheyennes believe that when a man dies his spirit leaves the body with the last breath of life. They say that the rope of the hangman does not permit the spirit to escape; that neither breath nor spirit can get past the rope. If the breath could pass, they argue, the man would not die. But as it cannot the soul must remain in the body. This, of course, prevents a hanged man from living in the Shadow Hills with his people who have passed. The hangman's rope has a deep terror for the red man because of this belief; and Head Chief and Young Mule refused to be hanged.

"The whole tribe agreed with them. The Cheyennes offered their all to save them. They would beggar themselves rather than have the spirits of the braves remain forever in their dead bodies. Runners were sent to offer every pony and every trinket to appease the demands of the white people. The Indians did not want battle, they said, but they would not consent to the hanging. They could not understand that property value would not pay for human life that had been taken.

"Matters were in a bad way, and the

agent had sent for soldiers. A troop of the first cavalry had been sent to Lame Deer. I was on my way there on the night of the twelfth. A half-breed Cheyenne was with me. His name was Pete. We were driving in a buckboard from Forsyth to the agency, having started early in the afternoon.

"Not far from Ashland we heard the war-drums beating, and Pete pulled the team down to a walk. 'By gar,' he said. 'Mebby she's mad now, dem Cheyenne. She's dance it war now.'

"The camp was near the road. I decided to go on. We drew near the fire and stopped the team. In the firelight two warriors were dancing to the beating drums and the voices of singers.

" 'See what's going on, Pete,' I said, and took the reins.

"The half-breed went to the camp. I

saw him enter the crowd about the dancers, and then I lost sight of him. The dance was wild. The Indians had all gathered; and while I waited I saw two more braves strip and commence to dance with the others. The singing increased in volume. The drums sounded louder, and the beating was faster. I was beginning to be worried, when I saw Pete coming. He was not alone. The chief was with him, and he was in no mood for chatting, either. He spoke to me and then to Pete, who repeated his words in English.

"Young Mule and Head Chief were going to die, he said. Word had been sent to Lame Deer that they would come in when morning came. They would not be hanged but would fight the soldiers until they died. I offered my hand to the chief but he refused it, and we drove away.

"'She's mad, de chief,' said Pete. 'Don't

like it for soldiers comin'. Better soldiers ain't comin', mebby.'

"'Maybe,' I said. But I was mighty glad they had come.

"We got to Lame Deer and found everyone awake and making ready for the Cheyennes. Many believed that a battle between the soldiers and the tribe was inevitable. I was somewhat afraid that it was, myself, because of the dance and the participation of others besides Head Chief and Young Mule.

"But morning broke calm and beautiful and quiet. At seven o'clock Indians began to appear on the hilltops. Men, women, and children decked out in Cheyenne finery sat upon every point within sight of the agency. The bugle sounded. The troop of cavalry formed in line of battle. The women and children of Lame Deer left the place for the hills near by. The Indian police came out and took their position with the soldiers. The stage was set. The amphitheatre was filled. Overhead the blue sky was without a cloud. And we waited. A fuzzy little yellow dog came out of the agency and trotted leisurely along in front of the soldiers. A cavalry horse nipped him on the back and he ran yelping down the road toward Ashland.

"Then a war-whoop drowned the dog's cries. I turned and saw two warriors come dashing down the hill toward the soldiers their beautiful war-bonnets trembling in the wind. Superbly mounted and riding like devils, they charged straight at the cavalry. Bang! A cavalry horse fell dead. Then there was a volley of shots; and Young Mule was down. His riderless horse whirled and left him not sixty yards from the foe.

"At fifty yards Head Chief turned his mount and rode along the line of cavalrymen, firing at them as he went. A soldier fell. A hundred bullets sought a mark in the Cheyenne; but he rode out of range, unharmed. Then again he turned his horse and rode back—back in the face of a troop of cavalry and the Indian police—back, I tell you, singing his death-song and banging away at the soldiers with his Henry rifle. A hail of bullets greeted him as he came, but he rode on singing and shooting to the very end of the line, untouched! With a yell of defiance he wheeled to come again; and met a dozen bullets. His horse, too, was killed.

"From off the hills where they had watched, the Cheyennes came for their dead. And chanting the tribal death-song to Head Chief and Young Mule, now safe in the Shadow Hills, they bore their bodies away.

"I believe a sneeze would have started a fight then. I was glad when they had gone."

WHAT FOLLOWED A SERMON

THE wind howled over the treeless stretches and when the sun went down snow-flurries pattered against the dirty panes of glass in the windows of the Marks and Brands saloon, sticking to the dingy corners of the sash and curling in little swirls on the boardwalk in front of the place. The small sign of a doctor swung in the gale with unearthly creaks and groans from the corner of a building near by, and lent lonesomeness to the deserted thoroughfare that fronted the right-of-way of the young Great Northern Railway. Dim yellow patches of light told the whereabouts of other places of business along the town's only street, and down near the river, dark and forbidding with its pile of wagon-wreckage and worn-out horseshoes, stood the Pioneer Blacksmith Shop. The light from the windows of Joe's Place fell full upon an open door of the shop and illuminated an array of cattle brands that had been burned upon it as proof of the craftiness of hand of Bill Hardesty, the blacksmith, who was dozing in a rickety chair in the saloon next to his place of business.

A pot-bellied stove, stuffed with soft coal, stood a little back of the centre of Joe's Place, and just outside the ring of light cast by a tin-shaded hanging lamp. Its puffy sides, reddened in spots, glowed in the gloom that was made deeper by the ring of light, and seemed to strain themselves in an attempt to give the comfort of heat to its owner's patrons.

Grouped about a round table, several men were intent in watching a game of stud-poker, evincing every whit as much mystery concerning the hole-card of the player nearest them as the interested one himself. A thin, blue, undulating cloud of tobacco smoke, with one quivering end bending downward in an effort to make connection with the draught of the stove, hung above the heads of the group, and almost hid a sign on the wall that warned "If You Cant Pay, Dont Play."

The town drunkard, ragged, red-eyed, and obliging, leaned against the bar with one shabby foot upon the rail before it, ready, nay anxious, to applaud the witticisms of Joe, the proprietor, or to fawn upon any who might loosen to buy, and at intervals surveyed himself in the fly-specked mirror back of the bar. Now and then he readjusted his hat, cocking it on the side of his tousled head, only to disapprove of its effect and change it to a new and different angle.

Joe, himself, fat to wheeziness, mopped the bar of the moisture left by the last round of drinks, and resting his dimpled elbows upon it, turned his attention to the poker game. A cuckoo-clock fluttered, a tiny door flew open, a wooden bird appeared; ding—cuck—oooo, sounded the bell and the bird in the reek of the room. Joe glanced at the wooden hands upon the wooden dial. "Eight-thirty," he said. "Number One's late, as usual." And the town drunkard laughed heartily.

"Expectin' somebody, Joe?" asked Pete Jarvis.

"Nope—just noticed she was more'n an hour late, an' I wanted to get a paper off'n her—that's all."

"It's a long time between, Joe. Fetch us somethin'," said Pete.

"What'll it be, boys?" asked Joe, bending a glance at the poker players.

"The same all 'round," said Pete. And Joe served them with whiskey.

"Give the Mascot a drink, too, Joe," said Pete, "an' have somethin' yerself."

Returning to the bar with the empty glasses, Joe set the whiskey bottle upon it for the town drunkard, who, filling a glass to the brim, turned, and with shaky hand that slopped the liquor, held it toward his benefactor a moment, then gulped its contents with a grimace. "Boooh!" he said, with a shake of his head. "Booohhh!"

"He jest natcherly hates that stuff, Pete," said Joe, sarcastically, as he wiped the bottle with his hand.

"Yep," said Pete, as he slyly peeked at the very corner of his hole-card, "yep, he shure does. He takes it for his wife's chilblains. Ante, Tom, an' pass the buck."

A whistle sounded above the shriek of the gale. "There she comes, at last," said Joe.

"Gimme a drink an' I'll go git you a paper off'n her," said the town drunkard.

"Get the paper first an' then have yer drink," said Joe, the child of experience, and the blear-eyed Mascot of Joe's Place sprang for the door. A gust of wind that made the hanging lamp flicker and swing dizzily screamed its defiance in the doorway, but grabbing his hat, the Mascot pushed his way into the night. The door shut with a crash, and the baffled gale shook it in impotent protest. "God!" said Joe, "I'd hate to be out in that. It's a blizzard, an' a good one." He crossed to the stove, and taking the coal scuttle, emptied its contents into the roaring flames. A jagged chunk that refused to enter the stove's door caromed about between the nose of the scuttle and the opening, then fell with a bang at the feet of the slumbering blacksmith, and a puff of black smoke shot from the overfed fire straight into his face.

"What the hell are you tryin' to do to

me? Want to barbecue me?" he cried, straightening himself in the chair. The laugh of the group at the table amused him and he turned, wiping the perspiration from his forehead with a red bandana handkerchief. "I'll buy," he said. "Joe, set 'em up. By gum, I was dreamin', I guess."

"I guess you must have been, Bill. I didn't go for to wake you, but——"

The screech of the brakes of Number One reached the room. The hiss of the steam from the overdue train added zest to the wind a moment, and then she was gone on her way, with her headlight groping through the blinding sheets of fine snow in the awful gale.

"Three calls five," said Pete. "Ye're shy one there, Tom." The chip was supplied and then the door opened. A gust of wind and a mist of snow preceded the Mascot, and behind him, with a small hand-bag in his gloved hand, was a stranger blinking in the light, and breathing the stuffy air of the place in gasps.

The town drunkard removed his hat and tiptoeing over the squeaking floor, led the way to the stove. "Better warm yourself, stranger," he said. "Here's your paper, Joe," and crossing to the bar he whispered behind his shaky hand, "Preacher—gimme that drink."

The stranger removed his gloves, unbuttoned his overcoat, and spread his thin hands to the heat of the stove. "Rather a disagreeable night, friends," he said, addressing the group at the table. There was no accusation in the glance that he gave with his words, although Pete was deftly gathering up the cards when he answered:

"Shure as hell is, stranger. Lookin' fer somebody, be you?"

"Oh, no. No one in particular. I am

the new minister of the Episcopal Church at Glasgow, and I want to hold services in your little city to-morrow, if a way can be found. Are there many members of our church here, do you know?"

Pete cleared his throat. "Well, there's John Tempy. He's somethin' or other, but darned if I know just what he is," he said, anxious to oblige.

Joe, fearing that unnecessary profanity might be indulged in, and not knowing that the stranger had told his business in town, hastened from behind the bar, wiping his hands upon his apron. He drew a chair to the stove. "Have a seat, pardner," he said, polishing the chair's seat with the apron. "Have a seat. He's a preacher, boys," and thus, having given due and timely warning, he returned to the bar, where he began to busy himself with the bottles and glasses there.

The poker players were cashing their chips and the Mascot, having sneaked his drink, had taken his place at the side of his discovery. Seeing that the game was about to be discontinued, and guessing the cause, the minister said: "Friends, I fear that I have interrupted your evening's entertainment, and let me say that while I am a minister of the Gospel, I am neither a bigot nor a cad. I know something of the ways of men, and to do my work in life, I must be a man among them, or fail. If you will tell me where I can find a place to sleep, I will leave you, for I am tired."

There was silence. Joe's cat, with bowed back, rubbed against the minister's leg, purring his welcome. Then Pete spoke. "John Tempy's would be the place, but Annie's sick. They think mebby she's comin' down with the smallpox, so you can't go there, I reckon. You can bunk with me, if ye're willin'."

"Of course—of course, I'm willing, and grateful to you; but do not let me disturb you here."

"I'll take him over," said the Mascot. "I'll take him over to Pete's if you'll——"

"All right—all right," broke in Joe. "You take him over." And buttoning his coat, the minister followed the town drunkard to Pete Jarvis's cabin, where, after building a fire, the Mascot left him, and hurried to the saloon for his reward.

"Had a notion to offer him a hot toddy," said Joe, as he set out the whiskey bottle for the Mascot.

"Bet he wouldn't a-taken it," said Tom Bodie.

"Bet you a hoss, he would uf," declared Bill Hardesty, the blacksmith. "I like that feller. He ain't no slouch nor four-flush."

"So do I like him," said Pete. "He don't look very well, to me. Where in hell's he goin' to preach at, do you reckon?"

"Don't know," said Joe. "He can't have Tempy's store, 'cause Tempy's bound to kick at havin' folks in there that way, an' you can't blame him. I'd—I'd—say, do you reckon he'd get sore if I offered him a chance to preach in here?"

"No," said Pete. "Not that feller. Besides, it's the only place, unless he goes to the Marks and Brands."

"Say, Pete," said Joe, "you tend bar a spell. I'll slip over to the Marks and Brands an' rib up a crowd for that old sport, an' we'll offer him this saloon in the mornin'. You can tell him, yerself, Pete, when you bed down. Needn't say nothin' 'bout me a-makin' this roundup, for there ain't more'n a dozen or twenty men in town, noway. An' there ain't no women folks outside of Tempy's women an' the Mascot's wife. They can't come, if they wanted to."

Joe untied his apron, put on his coat and

hat, and left the place. He battled his way against the storm to the Marks and Brands and entered. Under the glare of a sizzling gasolene lamp, a dozen men were playing cards, and several more were ranged about the billiard table upon which a drunken sheepherder lay asleep with several lighted candles, stuck in empty beer bottles, about him. His matted beard had had the attention of those about the table and was bedecked with yellow ribbons, filched from cigar packages, that had been tied in bows by unaccustomed fingers.

"Hey, Joe, can you sing?" called Kelly the Kid. "We got a dead one here."

"No, Kid, not a lick," said Joe. "Can I see you a minute, Jake?" and the proprietor of the Marks and Brands retreated to a corner with his visitor.

"Jake," said Joe, "there's a preacher in town."

"The hell!"

"Yes, an' he's bedded down at Pete Jarvis's."

"The hell!"

"Yep, an' he wants to hold services—to preach, you know, to-morrow, in this town; so I'm goin' to offer him my saloon to talk in—if he'll take it."

"Know him?"

"Nope, but he's all right. Come in on Number One, to-night. I'd like it if you an' the boys would come over to my place and hear that feller, a spell. Will you?"

"Shore—shore, Joe. 'Course, we'll come. What time?"

"I don't know, but I'll find out an' tell you."

"All right, Joe, we'll come—all of us," said Jake. "Have a little drink, Joe?" and the two walked to the bar, where they drank together.

"Come on—the house," called Joe, "an' have something on me." He laid a ten-dollar bill on the bar. Excepting the card-players and the sleeping sheepherder, everybody came to the bar and Joe told them his errand. "Jake an' me'd like it, bully, if you'd all come an' hear him, boys. It won't hurt you none, an' I do hate to see a man cold-decked. I don't want him to find out that I made this rustle, neither. It looks like leadin' from a sneak, kinder, but it's the only bet to get a crowd. Have another drink on me, boys, an' come an' hear Mr.—Mr.—well, I'm damned if I thought to ask him his name, but come anyway. He's a 'Piscopal. Good-night, Jake. Good-night, all. Be sure an' come over," and Joe bolted into the storm.

Reaching his own saloon, he did not put on his apron, but relieving Pete, called every one to the bar to regale themselves.

"Now, boys, don't forget to be on hand to-morrow, will you?" he said.

"We'll be Johnny-on-the-spot, Joe—all of us," declared Tom, as he drained his glass, "an' now I got to go to bed, myself." He left the saloon and one by one, a start having been made, the patrons of Joe's Place went to their beds.

Joe put out the hanging lamp, and took the money from the cash-drawer—the regular nightly warning to the town drunkard.

"Gimme a nightcap, Joe," whimpered the Mascot.

"Not a drop," said Joe. "You've had enough for to-night, an' you be on hand for that preachin' to-morrow or I'll break your damned neck!" He took a key from his pocket and led the way to the door. "Good-night, an' remember," he said, as the town drunkard went out into the blizzard.

Joe locked the door, and scratching a

match on his trousers, walked to the back of the saloon, shielding the blaze of the match with his hand. As the flame devoured the last of the stem he dropped it, and opened a door that let him into a shabby bedroom, where he lighted a lamp, and tearing the edges from a shirtbox, sat down on the bed. He fumbled in his vest pockets a moment, and then produced the stub of a pencil. With this he printed upon the white cardboard:

"THIS BAR IS CLOSED TILL HE'S DONE."

Then he undressed and got into bed. The blizzard searched the cracks in the building, for it was but a shack, and Joe listened to the storm for an hour before he slept.

Somebody was rattling the front door. Joe opened his eyes. It was morning and the bite of the cold made him shudder.

"Clink" went a bottle in the saloon; "pop" sounded the boards in the building, and again the door was shaken with a will. "All right—all right. In a minute!" called Joe to the impatient ones, and hurried into his clothes. With shoes unlaced and shirt yet unbuttoned, he unlocked the front door to admit Pete and the shivering Mascot. "Take a drink, boys, an' build a fire," he said, as he hurried back to complete his dressing.

"I told him, an' he's tickled to death," called Pete. "It's to be at ten-thirty."

"When you get that fire goin', Mascot, you go over an' tell Jake that the preachin's to be at ten-thirty, an' sweep out good an' plenty, too," called Joe from his bedroom. "Tell Jake I sent you. How cold is it, I wonder. I heard the bottles an' things a-poppin' in there, anyway. Is he up yet, Pete?"

"You bet he's up. Me an' him's had breakfast, too. He ain't no slouch, that feller, even if he is a preacher."

The blizzard had spent itself, but in its rage had left the world a stark, dead thing—all white and cold and still. The sun's light was blinding and the keen in the morning air stung Joe's face and stuck his eyelashes as he trudged through the small snow-drifts to the house of the Mascot, for breakfast. "Good morning, Mrs. Harris," he said as he stomped the snow from his feet and covered his ears with his hands. "Bad storm, wasn't it? The coffee smells mighty good this morning. I'm sorry you can't come to the preachin'."

"Well, I'm comin', Joe, even if it is in a saloon and even if I'm goin' to be the only woman there. This town's bad enough, God knows, without making it any worse in His eyes by not goin' to—to—to church when we have a chance," she said as she placed Joe's breakfast on the table.

"I'm glad you're comin', Mrs. Harris. It'll kinder hold the boys down, an' they won't deal him no cards from the bottom. Not that they would—but they might. These cakes is bully, Mrs. Harris. Everything's fine an' tastes good."

"You always say that, Joe."

"Well, it's always so, then. An' say, a man that owes me a bar bill, wants to pay me in meat an' spuds. I can't never get no real money out of him, noway. I told him I'd take 'em an' I'm goin' to fetch 'em over here, so's you can feed us with 'em—see? It'll be doin' me an' the feller, both, a favor."

Mrs. Harris cleared her throat. "Joe," she said, "there's been a lot of bills you collected that way—bad debts, you called 'em. The worst of it is, you won't let it go on your board, an' it makes me feel that me an' Lem's livin' off'n you."

"Well, you ain't," said Joe. "I'd starve in this town, if it wasn't for this place here, an' besides, I'd lose the bills I get in that way, if I didn't have no place to slough the truck. Don't you worry, Mrs. Harris, there's plenty profit in it, for me. I got to be goin', an' get ready for the big doin's," and fearing that his bounty might call forth more thanks, he left the house.

Mrs. Harris, a woman of fifty, turned from the breakfast-table with the dishes in her hands, and sighed, as she deposited them in the kitchen. "If there ever was a good, honest man, it's Joe Prentiss," she said. Then she washed and put away the dishes and tidied herself to attend the preaching.

Joe, back at the saloon, which had been swept clean by Pete and the Mascot, went to his room, and bringing out the cardboard, set up his sign back of the bar. "That goes as it looks," he said. "Have you told Jake the time of the preachin', Mascot?"

"Not yet. Gimme a drink an' I'll go now."

"Well, help yourself. It's the last ye'll get till the sermon's done. Now, go an' tell Jake, an' everybody you see. Tell 'em—tell 'em—well, tell 'em, after it's all over with, the drinks will be on me—after the preacher's gone."

An hour afterward men began to arrive. They came singly and in pairs, and sheepishly tried to make light of the affair, but reading Joe's sign, and noting the serious look on his face, they soon left off any attempt at hilarity, and when Mrs. Harris entered, Pete said: "I'll go an' git him, now, Joe."

"Take that dog out with you, Pete," said Joe, and his voice was solemnly pitched. "Have this chair, Mrs. Harris."

As the woman seated herself, instinctively every hat in the place was removed, and a stillness crept upon the company there. The sunlight streamed in through the windows and Tom Bodie rubbed the lighted end of his cigar against his chair, to put it out.

"Good morning, friends," said the cheery voice of the minister. His eyes glanced about the room and fell upon the sign back of the bar. Then his gaze sought the proprietor, just a moment, but Joe's eyes were riveted upon the floor. The stranger shook hands with every one there, and spoke especially to Mrs. Harris, thanking her for her presence. Then, for an hour he preached of life, and the simple-heartedness of those before him inspired him to touch them deeply. There was no sting, no chastisement, in his words. They only felt the man's thanks for their presence there. With his appeal for righteousness was coupled an acknowledgment of their hospitality and their respect for him, a stranger, preaching to men of many creeds on a bitter winter morning. "When we shall have known each other for a little time, I feel sure that mutual good will come to us, for I need your help and your lessons to aid me. And perhaps I may help you, not only as a minister, but as a friend," he said in closing.

Joe, hat in hand, began to tiptoe among the men. The clink of silver drew the attention of the minister, who was talking to Mrs. Harris.

"Just one moment, please," he called. Joe stopped in his tracks, his fat face red to the ears.

"I appreciate your kindness, but let us wait until we have established ourselves in some organized effort in church work before we take up a collection. Then we shall have a use—a direct cause for the money. Don't you think that would be the better way?"

"I reckon it would, mebby," said Joe. "You can come here any time you want to, pardner."

"Thank you, and all of you," said the minister, as he walked outside with Mrs. Harris.

Joe took down the sign from behind the bar, and tying his apron about his waist, said: "Come on, everybody, an' have somethin'. I am mighty glad you come."

"Boys," he said, after the drinking had ceased, "that man said a whole lot to us that is true. An' he didn't fork no high hoss, neither. I hope he comes again."

"Me, too," said Pete.

"Now," continued Joe, "this town *is* tough. The boys come in off'n the range, shoot up the place, an' fight like hell. You all know it an' I know it. We ain't decent an' quiet like we ort to be. How many women is they in this town? Just four, countin' a couple of kids. I ain't countin' them that's over across the river; not but what they're as good as the most of *us*, but you can't count 'em along with the others, hardly. No more'n you can count us along with that preacher. I think we'd better organize ourselves, an' elect somebody judge. Call him a police judge, or any kind of a judge; as long as we all back him up in what he says, it don't make no difference what we call him. Let him fine hell out of fighters. Let's all be for law an' order in this town from now on. I don't have to point out the times when we needed 'em both mighty bad."

"The town ain't incorporated, Joe," said a voice.

"I don't care if it ain't," said Joe. "We are able to run it an' nobody's a-goin' to kick if we copper all fight-bets. Let's appoint somebody judge right now while we're all here to have a hand in it. Then when anybody gets fighty an' wants to go to war, we'll arrest him, an' the judge will fine him good an' plenty. Enough to take the fight out'n him."

"Where's the jail, Joe?" asked Pete.

"We can use the root-house," said Joe. "But we won't want a jail if they find out they're goin' to be fined for fighting. That's our big trouble—is the fights. Let's try it, boys."

"All right," said Pete. "I nominate Bill Hardesty for judge."

The blacksmith protested. "I don't know nothin' 'bout law. I'm busy an' I won't have nothin' to do with——"

"All in favor, say I," called Joe. "The I's have it. Judge Hardesty, have a drink with your feller citizens."

That afternoon when Number Three stopped at the station, two young men got off the train, and crossing the street to Joe's Place, stood for a moment, watching the departing coaches, ere they entered.

"Can you tell us where Mr. McLeod's ranch is?" asked one of the young men of Joe.

"—Sandy McLeod?" asked Joe.

"Mr. Kenneth McLeod," said the young man. "He's a sheepman."

"That's Sandy," said Joe. "Yes, he's forty miles north of here. Used to be the old Bar Four, cow ranch. I used to ride for that iron, myself. You bet I know where it is."

"Is he in town to-day?"

"No," said Joe. "Have a little smile?"

"We don't drink, thank you," said the young man.

"Well, stay right with it," said Joe.

"Make yourselves to home here. Sandy'll likely be in, if he's expectin' you."

"We are going to herd sheep for him," explained the young man, "my brother and I. We are from Ohio. Mr. McLeod expects us." And Sandy came that evening, and took the young herders away.

June had come with its soft leaves and prairie flowers. The range, an endless rolling stretch of tender green, fattened the great herds of cattle and sheep, and with its gentle breezes and bird song, proclaimed itself a bountiful paradise.

The clang of the blacksmith's hammer resounded through the town, and before the shop where Bill Hardesty sweated, were tied many horses awaiting their turn for new shoes. A hobo, tramping his way through the land, had been hired temporarily as helper, and so throughout the long days and even into the night, the blacksmith labored; not only for the pay in money, but to oblige. A pair of bluebirds, ignoring the noise of Bill's trade, had builded a nest in a box under the eaves of the roof of the shop with much fluttering and carolling.

The steel rails on the slightly graded right-of-way reached hungrily toward the horizon east and west, shimmering in the sun's heat, dipping mysteriously into the phantom waters of a mirage-lake; then out and on again until they seemed to meet where the sky came down to the grass-tops. Bending over his anvil, a white-hot horseshoe in his tongs, Bill's hammer descended once, and then was hurled at Tempy's tomcat that was creeping toward a bluebird upon the ground. Stuffing the horseshoe back into the fire, he went outside to recover his hammer, and met Pete Jarvis. "Damn that cat," he said as he rubbed the face of his hammer against his leathern apron. "Say, Pete, what'll I do with that fine-money? I got sixty dollars now. I'll kill that cat of Tempy's, yet."

Pete thought a moment, removed his hat and scratched his head. "Bill," he said, "you ought to have a liberry."

"Liberry?" said Bill, still watching the cat.

"Yes," said Pete, "a law liberry. It would look a heap more reg'lar, Bill. Send away an' get you some law books. Get you a liberry."

"I wouldn't have no idee where to send, Pete. You take the darn money an' send an' git them books for me, will you?"

"Shure—I'll do the best I can," and taking the sixty dollars, Pete went over to Joe's Place and bought a drink. That night he spent the money with the unsuspecting judge and the rest who happened in. It was a glorious evening, and Joe wondered at Pete's sudden affluence, but it was without his province to ask questions; so the sixty dollars went into his till.

The library came: donated codes by the State of Montana, in the interest of law and order. Pete took the two heavy volumes to the blacksmith shop. "Here they be, Bill," he said.

"Say, you don't reckon I'll ever read 'em, do you?" asked Bill, as he rubbed the soil from his hands and began to turn the thin pages.

"Hell, no, but it's the looks of 'em here, Bill. When we fetch a man here an' he sees them books, he'll dig up easier—heaps easier. Ain't they fine—them books? I'll make you a box to keep 'em in, where they'll show," and he did.

"Shore cost money, don't they?" said Bill, as he surveyed the books in the box on the dingy wall. "Well, the disturbers bought 'em. We didn't. It was their own money that paid for them books as shore's the devil's a pig."

It was not long until the fund, exhausted by the purchase of the library, began to sprout anew, however. Pete's readiness to arrest, and Bill's anxiety to fine disturbers of the peace, had nourished the new beginning into something quite substantial, when, one day, in haling a drunken cow-puncher before his honor in the blacksmith shop, the self-appointed city marshal was roughly handled.

After the cowboy had been relieved of ten dollars and had gone his way swearing vengeance, Pete wiped the blood from his bruised nose upon the back of his hand and gazed at the stain through a rapidly closing eye. "Jest look at me, Bill," he said. "That feller was on the prod an' went to war from the jump."

"Well, he paid, didn't he?" asked Bill, as he laid the greenback in the box with the fines and placed a toe-calk upon it.

"He didn't pay me," declared Pete. "I don't know who I'm workin' for, an' right here's where I find out. I ain't goin' to tie into every drunk in this town single-handed, no more, without knowin' whose iron I'm ridin' for, Bill. It's too damn hard on the eyes. Nobody works for nothin'—not even preachers, an' I won't, neither."

"I don't git no pay, do I?" asked Bill.

"You get it all, don't you? An' your job ain't liable to leave yer relations a-wonderin' if you was buried decent, is it? Hell, man, let's divide. Let's cut it two ways. I round 'em up an' you brand 'em. That's only fair, ain't it?"

Bill's eyes opened wide. "Say," he said, stepping close to Pete and looking into his battered face, "is this *our* money—this here fine-money?"

"'Course it is," said Pete. "We work for it, don't we? Who else is in on it, I'd like to know? What we earn is ours, ain't it? It would be a hell of a world if it wasn't, wouldn't it?"

"I didn't know whose money it was, Pete. If it's ours, I'll divide, of course. I'll cut it with you." And he divided the fund on the spot. "Let's go over to Joe's. I'm done for to-day, anyhow."

"What's the matter with this town, Joe?" asked Jake, of the Marks and Brands saloon, of the proprietor of Joe's Place, one day in the fall. "If it wasn't for Pete Jarvis and Bill Hardesty, an' a few of the regulars, we'd starve. They don't seem to come into this town any more—I mean the cow-punchers and the sheepherders. The town's dead, awful dead."

"I've noticed it, too, but mebby business

will pick up now that the busy season's over on the range and ranches. Tempy's kickin', too, so I reckon it's an even break all around," said Joe. "But I've noticed it.—Number Two's wrecked. Hear about it?"

"No."

"Yes, she's in the ditch somewhere west of here. Won't be no train till to-morrow." The sound of singing came to them from Joe's Place, and Jake bent an inquiring glance upon the proprietor.

"Drummers," he said. "One of 'em sells shoes an' the other shirts. They wanted to get out on Number Two, but she's wrecked, so now they're havin' a spree."

"Who's them two, there?" and Jake nodded toward the two young men who had arrived in the early spring and had gone to work for McLeod.

"They been herdin' for Sandy. First time they been in town since last spring.

Must be fairly fat now, but they don't drink—neither of 'em."

"Well, I got to be goin'. I hope things pick up," said Jake, as he turned toward the Marks and Brands.

Joe entered his own saloon, where "Bonnie Annie Laurie" was being butchered by the two travelling salesmen, with their arms tight around the town drunkard. The two young men, having visited the station, had learned the fate of Number Two, and having no other place in which to loaf, came to Joe's.

"Welcome, s-s-strangers. Wel—come. Have a dddrink," and the salesman wearing a derby hat hurried to lead the young men to the bar.

"No, thanks; we don't drink," said one of the boys.

The salesman stopped, let go of the hand he held, and swaying slightly, looked earnestly at the speaker a moment.

"Tha—sa goo wand—don drink. I—I nev heard tha-wan f-fore. S—s-new—bran' nnew. Ha-ha-ha—don d-drink. I'm g-goin' mem-member zat-wan. Come on and have som-som-sing wiz sus, fr-friends tha don-don drink."

"No, thank you."

"I in-inshist."

"No."

"Wan-na in-insult me an' my f-f-frens? Hey, wa-na?"

"No, but we don't drink."

"I inshist. Barkeep, set 'em."

"No."

Wildly the fellow struck at the young man, and in the twinkling of an eye, there was a fight—three against two; but the two were sober. Chairs were broken, a window crashed, and Joe was running from behind the bar when Pete entered.

"What's a-goin' on here!" he yelled.

"Stop it!" and he struck right and left with his fists. With Joe's help, the battle was soon ended.

"Come on, all of you," said Pete. "You're under arrest."

The prisoners, all talking at once, followed Pete to the blacksmith shop, where Bill was fighting a broncho and swearing at the top of his voice. The interior of the shop was hidden by a cloud of dust when Pete entered with his prisoners. The broncho, at last conquered, was breathing heavily, blowing dust from the floor at every gasp, when, hearing the babble of the visitors, the terrified horse struggled fiercely, thrashing his head against the dirt floor of the place. "Whoah, damn you. Lay still!" and the perspiring blacksmith turned to survey the group of callers.

"Can't monkey with 'em now, Pete. I'm busy. Got to git some shoes on that ——

—— ornery brute there. He's wilder'n a grizzly's dream an' meaner'n a coyote. Fetch 'em back by an' by. What's the charge?"

"Fightin', judge," said Pete.

"All of 'em?"

"Yes, the whole caboodle."

"If these two fellows had taken a drink when we asked them to, there wouldn't have been any row. They are the real disturbers, judge," said the salesman with the derby hat, suddenly sobered. "We were having a good time, when these two butted in and insulted us."

"That's the truth," said Pete. "Them two's to blame for this, judge. I don't aim to take no sides. They been herdin' sheep for Sandy McLeod since last spring an' ain't been to town once in that whole time. Not since they come to the country."

The judge caught the suggestion in Pete's

words. "Whoah, damn you," he cried, as he turned to tighten a rope that held the broncho. Then facing the prisoners he asked: "Did you refuse to drink when the gentleman asked you to?"

"We don't drink," said both the young men.

"Well, you disturbed the peace of this town—that's all. I fine you twenty-five dollars apiece."

"There's no law on earth that enforces a man to drink against his will," declared one of the young men, hotly. "I'll——"

"Pay up or git locked up. I'm busy, an' that's the law in this country. It's in that there biggest book—about the middle, some place. You can read it fer yerself, if you want to— Whoah! damn you, whoah!"

"Of course it's the law," declared the salesman. "I live in this State and I know, judge."

"Pay up or I'll throw you in," said Pete, and the fifty dollars were paid.

Night came, and then the day, which brought the passenger-train headed East. The young men and the travelling salesmen got aboard without speaking, and Joe went over to the Marks and Brands. "Jake," he said, "Pete an' Bill's goin' too strong. It's hurtin' the town. Let's us get together an' fire 'em."

CRANKS

THE tamaracks were turning yellow when Jim Turner and Sank Whetford began cutting logs with which to build their cabin on Indian Creek. The site chosen for the cabin was a natural park—early to catch the sun's light in the morning, and blessed with his last rays ere he bade good-by to the range at evening. The dark firs and spruce trees retained their usual hues, and in the golden sunlight of Montana's fall, made a fitting background for the brilliant orange of the tamarack needles, so soon to fall and mark each deer-trail a gilded way.

Jim and Sank were trappers, and had spent their lives apart from other men. It was during a spree in the early summer that they had met and discovered deep friendship, and they had contrived to spend much time together ever since. At Jake's saloon, or at the store at the Crossing, they had spent many hours planning to winter together, and Indian Creek had been decided upon, months before. Jim's camp had been a mile up the stream from the store; while Sank's tent had adorned the landscape a mile below it. One day Jim said: "Sank, better move up to my camp. We kin plan an' talk a heap better. I'd like fer to have ye near me, anyhow."

"All right, Jim," said Sank. "I'll ketch up the hosses in the mornin' an' move up." And he did.

He pitched his tent near that of Jim's, and one fire served both. Each had his own tent, and Jim cooked and ate his meals when and as he pleased. So did Sank. The friendship ripened with the passing of summer, and when the fall began to turn the leaves yellow, and the ducks and the geese were flying southward, Jim and Sank bought their supply of grub, ammunition, and tobacco, and set out for Indian Creek.

The sound of their axes woke the sleeping echoes in the wilderness, and log after log of the dry, straight, and plentiful tamaracks were dragged to the growing cabin, until it was completed. Then Sank took the horses back to the valley for the winter, and while he was away, Jim put the finishing touches to the interior of the cabin, building a fireplace in a corner.

When, ten days later, Sank returned from the valley, Jim led him to the fireplace, and pointing with pride at the fire that was snapping gayly there, said: "See her draw, Sank. Green wood's jest duck soup fer it."

"She's shore some ol' honey, Jim," said Sank. "I brought up a little drop of liquor; hev a little snort?"

"Shore I will. Here's to us, Sank," and Jim took a long pull from the flask. "What do ye think of them shelves, and our rifle-rack, hey, pardner?"

"Bully, Jim, bully. Guess I'll hev a little smile, myself," and Sank took his turn at the flask. Then he set it upon one of the new shelves. "Comfortable an' fine's frog's hair, in here," he declared, and Jim's eyes glistened at Sank's every approving glance.

"Good range where ye left the hosses, Sank?" asked the proud Jim.

"You bet, an' I pulled off them shoes that was on that roan hoss of yours. Reckoned you'd want 'em off," said Sank.

"Bully fer you. I was intendin' to ask ye to take 'em off, but I forgot it. When a feller has a pardner that's like you, he don't have to think of everything himself. You know what ye're doin' all the time," said Jim, as he filled his pipe. "Ye're a born mountainman, Sank. That's what you be. I'm most awful damned glad I met up with ye," and Jim offered his horny hand to his partner, who shook it warmly.

"Dang yer ol' hide, Jim," said Sank, as he drew his hand across his eyes, "I been as lonesome as a bullfrog in Lake Superior, in these hills, but it's over with, Jim. It's a blind trail now. Let's finish that flask an' turn in, pardner. We been a-trapesin' these hills alone fer twenty-five years. Now we're pardners fer keeps, me an' you."

There was a scramble to build the morning fire and cook the breakfast. "You mustn't try to do it all, Sank," said Jim.

"Don't cal'late to," said Sank. "There's plenty fer the both of us to do, I reckon."

After breakfast they began cutting wood for use when the snows should come, and day after day the pile grew until, a week later, Jim declared there was enough to last till the grass started in the spring. "I'm shore tickled we met up with each other, pardner," said Jim, as he stuck his axe in a stump near the cabin. "Never did find a man I could git along with—that wasn't a crank."

"Well, I shore ain't no crank," declared Sank.

"I know ye ain't, an' I ain't, neither. Not by a damned sight. I don't like 'em. I can tell 'em, always. I know 'em soon's I set my eyes on 'em. They're like the wood-mice—all look alike. There's Hank Jennings—hell, I'd as soon camp with a he-grizzly bear as him. Always a-growlin' 'round, an' as lazy as a chilled rattlesnake."

"I started to winter, once, with ol' Bill Henry," said Sank, whittling some shavings with which to build a fire in the cabin.

"Oh my!—ha-ha-ha!" Jim's sides shook with laughter.

"Yes, I did," confessed Sank, lighting the shavings.

"Ye poor devil! Oh, Lord! Bill Henry! How long did it last?"

"Oh, 'bout a month, I reckon. That buck was fat, wasn't he?" said Sank, as he cut steaks from the hind quarter of a fat deer.

Then, one night, it snowed. A foot of it covered the mountains. "She's here, Jim," said Sank, as he opened the cabin door at daylight. "About a foot of it. Seems good, too."

After breakfast they took their rifles and set out to look for sign. Jim went west and Sank headed toward the east. At night they returned to the cabin in fine spirits. "Not much stirrin' yet. Too fresh. But I found some marten tracks, and there's lots of deer an' elk," said Jim.

"I run across some lynx tracks, an' seen where several marten had crossed that big gulch, east of here," confided Sank. "I reckon we'll pick up a pretty good ketch," and he began to hum a tune, as he hung up his rifle. "Saw a big band of elk, but they was too far from camp to kill."

"We'd better do a little killin' for bait, one of these days," said Jim. "I killed a buck down near the creek, where it cuts the trail, this mornin'. I fetched the hind quarters in with me. I reckon I'll set a few traps to-morrow."

"Me, too. They don't do no good in camp," said Sank, who began cooking supper.

Jim went to the creek for water and then whittled shavings for kindling in the morning, humming a bar or two from "Dixie," as the keen blade of his knife shaved the pitchy stick.

After supper, they lighted their pipes and told of their experiences and of the doings of friends and foes, until Jim yawned. "Well, Sank, I guess I'll turn in. I reckon I'll set a few traps in that big cedar swamp below here, in the mornin'. You shore do snore like a choked bull, but it don't bother me none."

"Me, snore? I didn't never know it. Nobody never said so. I reckon I must git to layin' on my back. But snorin' don't keep me awake. If it did, I'd hev to move camp, 'cause you kin hit the fastest gait I ever heared in all my camp-kettle career."

"If I snore, I never heared of it," said Jim. "But mebby I do. This ol' bunk feels good to-night. I'm kinder leg-weary," and he rolled over to sleep.

Sank went to the door and looked out. "She's snowin' agin, an' it looks like a good one, too. Booo! it's cold. I'll put that big chunk on the fire." He watched the blaze leap upon the fresh fuel, and then turned in. Almost as soon as he had tucked the blankets about him, Jim's snoring filled the cabin. "Oh, no, you don't snore, ner nothin'. Ye sleep jest like a little baby with a belly full, you do, Gosh! I'd hate to be like that—snortin' an' snappin', an' grittin' my teeth. But go to it, old timer; ye won't keep me awake none."

When Sank opened the door in the morning, the snow was piled high, and the air was full of more that was falling. "Say! We can't move to-day, Jim," he cried. "Biggest fall of snow I ever seen. Must be four feet deep right now an' still it's comin' down. We'll have to wait for it to settle some."

Jim was kindling the fire. "That's bad," he said. "I figured on gittin' out some of them traps to-day."

"Well, if they was set now, we'd only have to dig 'em out an' set 'em agin. It'll take a while for this snow to settle so's a man can snowshoe a mile a week."

They tramped a trail to the creek and wallowed a way to the woodpile, and still the snow kept falling. Each morning these trails had to be made anew. The sky was still black and the silence of the wilderness of snow oppressed them, cooped in the cabin as they were. "It's a week, to-day," growled Sank. "We're snowed in like a couple o' bears in a cave. Wish we hadn't come to this dod-rotted country. Dog-on fools, both of us."

"No use growlin'," said Jim. "'Tain't my fault because it snows."

"You picked the country, though."

"I did not pick the country. You said there'd be fur here, an' I agreed, didn't I?"

"Well, breakfast's ready," growled Sank.

"Forgit to salt the meat?" asked Jim.

"No. I didn't forgit nothin'."

"You didn't forgit to snore last night. I'll swear to that," said Jim, reaching for the frying-pan.

"Me, snore? I set up in bed listenin' to *you* eat 'em alive, last night. Pass the salt."

"Git the damned salt, if ye want it. Ye ain't helpless altogether, be ye? Don't hev to put on no airs, here. Why don't ye cook yer own meals, if ye don't like my cookin'? I kin cook to suit *me*. I did it long before I ever knowed *you*, an' now ye're a-kickin' all the damned time."

"That's jest what I'll do. I'll cook my own meals."

"Well, do it, an' see if I care."

After breakfast, Jim began stringing a rope across the cabin, whistling as he worked. After the rope was secure, he sewed blankets to it so they divided the cabin into two parts, leaving a trifle more than half toward the fireplace. Then he divided the grub and moved half of the supplies back of the blanket wall. There was no conversation, and the snow was still falling while he worked.

Sank watched him but offered no suggestions. Finally he heard Jim digging a hole in the ground behind the partition. He was using an axe in the digging and Sank wondered, but did not break the silence. When Jim went to the creek for water, Sank looked behind the blanket. Jim was going to make mud with which to build a fireplace, and was digging a hole in the cabin to get the dirt. "Hu!" muttered the spy, as the workman returned with the water.

Jim toiled all day. Having first chopped a hole in the roof so that the smoke of future fires might find a vent, he smeared the cabin logs, in the corner under the hole, with a deep coating of mud. But it was night before he ventured to build a fire in the makeshift fireplace. Then it was a small, weak blaze that furnished barely enough heat to cook his supper. Smoke came over the blankets, hung over Sank's head lazily, and then was finally drawn up the chimney of the old fireplace, but Sank did not mention it. He ignored it, or seemed to. He cooked and ate his supper alone. Then he went to bed. But Jim didn't retire. He began chopping a door on his side of the partition, and each blow of the axe shook the cabin, so that sleep was impossible.

"It's better'n his snorin'," mumbled Sank. "Damned crank."

It was late when the chopper finished, but at dawn he was up and at it again. Three days of torture passed before the new quarters suited Jim, and then the snow had settled somewhat. He took his traps and set out, crossing Sank's trail in the snow. "Hu!"

he said, "the crank's out already. My, but he's a rustler, ain't he?"

When night came, Jim returned. There was fire in Sank's part of the cabin, and the smell of frying meat had penetrated to beyond the partition. "Whew!" said Jim, audibly. "Whew! stink a coyote away from a dead hoss," and he left the door of the new quarters wide open. Then he built a fire against the logs in the corner where he had plastered the mud.

> "Bring the good old bugle, boys,
> We'll have another song.
> We'll sing it as we used to sing it,
> Fifty thousand strong."

Sank was singing. Sank had been a Union soldier, and Jim and his people had sided with the South.

"Noise," growled Jim, under his breath. "Nothin' but disturbance from dawn to dark." Then he rattled his tin plates noisily, and let a frying-pan fall loudly. The singing ceased. Profane words reached Jim's ears from over the blankets. "Rebel crew," he thought he heard, as he set his coffee-pot on the fire, in a quarrelsome mood. After supper he built up his fire, and sat before it. He could hear Sank snoring in comfort. It made him furious. He seized his rifle —BANG!

The snoring stopped, and he heard Sank get out of his bunk. "Dod-rot a mountain rat," growled Jim, measuring his voice that Sank might hear the words. "I'll fix 'em." Then, with a satisfied smile, he turned in.

When the morning came, the weather was extremely cold. All night long the logs in the cabin had popped in the frost, and the trees in the forest checked and snapped in the bitter blast from the north. Jim built a big fire in the corner, and went to the creek for water. The wind had drifted the snow, and the trail to the creek was full. Sank had not been out yet, so Jim had to tramp and wallow through to the water. It took quite a time, and then, after reaching the creek, he was obliged to cut through the ice in order to get the water. When he at last reached the cabin, the logs back of the mud were afire. The cabin was filled with smoke, but the neighbor had not interfered. At a glance, Jim saw the danger and threw the water upon the blaze, but it was not enough to check the fire, that had gained a good start in the dry tamarack logs. Desperately Jim fought the fire with the axe, but with a roar, the flames flared up, lighting the dark cabin and filling the place with sparks that floated over the partition. These brought Sank's tousled head through the blanket partition. Jim stared at him a moment, helplessly. "I'm burnin' *my* half of this damned cabin. You kin do what you please with yours," and he began to drag his belongings out into the deep snow.

THE FLYING DUTCHMAN

THE sun's first rays were just pricking their way through the breaks of the Missouri River on a keen December morning in the sixties when a lone Indian crept to a hilltop and looked down at the stream. His gaze was directed to a heavy grove of cottonwood trees opposite Cow Island from which two thin streaks of smoke were rising in the still morning air. There was a jumble of voices—white men's voices—in the grove, and other sounds as strange to the wilderness. They held the red man's attention; but ever and anon his eyes followed the thin trails of blue smoke that ascended in straight lines to the height of the bluffs along the river, where both bent gracefully downward and went lazily away on the gentle eastern breeze that was stirring over the plains above the stream.

Down by the river a steamboat was unloading the last of her freight consigned to Fort Benton, one hundred and thirty miles up the river. The boat had been hard aground four times on the day she had tied up at the bank, and her captain had given up the struggle. He could go no farther. The water was too shallow. The cargo from St. Louis must be unloaded to await the coming of freighters with bull teams, who would haul it to its destination. The season was late. Ice had already formed along the banks of the river, and where the eddies quieted the current it had crept far out toward the centre of the stream; so that there was need of haste if the boat would reach the lower river before the freeze-up.

As the sunlight touched the naked treetops in the grove, the trails of smoke increased in volume, a whistle disturbed the echoes with its blast, a bell tinkled sweetly, and white steam spurted from the exhaust pipes to mingle with the smoke from the steamer's stacks. There was a hissing, churning sound as the boat backed away from the bank and turned her nose down the stream toward St. Louis.

The Indian stood erect on the hilltop as the steamer swung around the bend in the river below Cow Island, her paddle-wheel churning the water into white foam as if she were anxious to escape the northern winter whose breath was in the air. Little tinkling noises came from the thin ice along the shores as the water, violently disturbed by the steamboat, broke it in pieces. Now and then a thin sheet would be thrown upward and, landing upon the unbroken ice, would slide over the surface with a scraping sound that only ice can make. Often these thin sheets would skate merrily over the undisturbed ice and land unbroken against the bank, where, turned sidewise to the rising sun, they reflected his light like a thousand flashing mirrors.

At last she was gone. The steamer *Sparrow Hawk* had withdrawn from the wilderness with her civilization. And the Indian, descending the hill a little way, mounted his pony and rode away.

Down in the grove by the river two white men stood silently gazing in the direction the boat had taken. The water had quieted; the broken ice still reflected the sun's light from the blue sky; but for long after the steamer had disappeared the men stood still and followed with their eyes the smoky way of the *Sparrow Hawk* as she widened the distance between them and their erstwhile mates.

"Ha, ha, ha!" laughed one of the men at

last. His breath was white in the air, and his laugh was harsh and unnatural.

His startled companion faced him. "What are you laughing at, Van?" he asked.

"Nothing, I guess. I just thought what fools we are to have volunteered to guard these goods till the bullwhackers come for them, that's all. It may be a month, and it may be never. I should have known better. I've been up the river before now. The Indians are bad, and if there is anything I am afraid of it's an Indian."

His name was Van Renssler, and he spoke with a slight foreign accent. Turning, he surveyed the big pile of bales and boxes the boat had left. "Not a drop of whiskey or high wines in all of that," he said disgustedly. "The wood-hawks will come—once—and then go away. If we had whiskey, we'd have a few visitors, but without it we'll have none at all. Let's fix up a camp."

"There's plenty of grub, anyhow," said the other, as he unrolled a wall tent. "We can make a comfortable camp here, and wood's handy."

"Yes, the camp will be comfortable if only the Indians don't find us," replied Van Renssler, cutting a cottonwood pole. "I saw a camp of wood-hawks below here about fifteen miles, I should think. They might call on us, but unless we have whiskey they will not call a second time. I know them."

"I haven't seen an Indian, though. Have you?" asked the other man.

"No—not one," said Van. "But they're here, or close to here. This is the land of the Blackfeet. Now! up she comes." And they raised the wall tent and pegged it to the slightly frozen ground.

"There she is," said Van. "Now we'll build a fire in front of it, and then one of us will go out and kill some meat. Hey, pardner?"

"I guess so," said the other, whose name was Tom Spencer. "But we oughtn't to do much shooting, I reckon. You'd better go. I'll finish making the camp comfortable."

Van set out in search of meat, and Tom, left alone, began to make the tent snug. Time went so swiftly that the sun had passed the meridian before he noticed it. He lighted his pipe and viewed his work with satisfaction.

"Haloo-oo!"

Tom started. The hail came from over the river, and he seized his rifle and listened.

"Haloo-oo, over there!"

"Hello!" answered Tom. "Make a raft and come over."

"Got any whiskey?" came the voice from over the river.

"Not a drop. But come over and visit," called Tom.

He heard several voices in conversation,

and then: "Too much work to get across," came to him from the other bank.

Three men—wood-hawks—now came down to the river's edge and looked across at the pile of freight doubtingly. Then, waving farewell, they turned away.

The shadows were long when at last Van returned with a fat antelope. Tom told him about the wood-hawks.

"I knew it," said Van. "They're the only white men within a hundred and thirty miles, but they despise so cheap an outfit, and I don't blame them. It's getting colder. There's plenty of game, though. I saw lots of antelope and several deer. Let's skin out this buck. He's fat as butter."

The sun set in a clear sky. Night came on with its big round moon, and in the beauty of the moonlight among the leafless trees, Van and Tom forgot their loneliness. They watched the shadows creep across the river where the ice was forming anew, and heaped dry wood upon the fire, until Van yawned. "I suppose we ought to stand guard, but let's take a chance to-night and sleep," he said.

"All right," agreed Tom. "I don't believe there's an Indian near here, anyhow."

There was an abundance of blankets, and the bed was warm. In the last flicker of firelight both men turned over and slept soundly.

Next morning the river was frozen nearly across, and from the open way of the waters a mist was rising in the bright morning air. Van went to the river for water, and returning, filled the coffee-pot and put it on the fire.

"Hey! Tom," he called. "Get up and hear the little birds sing their praises."

It was night again before they realized it. In the firelight they told their stories and, again omitting to stand guard, went to bed.

But each day was like the others. The stories played out. Weeks passed, and each night the wolves howled dismally. Silence had come to them and with it greater loneliness settled upon the camp at Cow Island. Days and even nights passed with scarcely a spoken word between them.

"I don't believe anybody wants this damned truck," growled Tom, as he surveyed the pile in the growing gloom of night.

"Neither do I," said Van. "Most likely nobody knows it's here. Give me that list and let me look it over."

"Here it is," and Tom handed his partner a half-dozen sheets of paper. "I'm going to turn in," he added, as Van took the papers.

Van threw wood on the fire and seated himself before it with the list of freight in his hands.

The river had frozen solid. Along the

banks the ice was smooth and clear, but out in the middle of the stream where the swifter water interfered with the work of the frost it was bulged and rough. No snow had fallen, but the weather had steadily grown colder; and Van shivered as finally he folded the sheets of paper with a sigh. Throwing a last glance at the dark pile of freight, he followed Tom into the tent and slept.

When morning came, Van had the fire started and was prowling among the boxes, which were consigned to hardware dealers at Fort Benton, Helena, and Virginia City.

"What the dickens are you looking for, Van?" called Tom from the tent.

"Skates," growled Van. "If I had a pair of skates I'd go to Fort Benton and get us some whiskey. It's only four more days till Christmas; but there ain't no skates in the hardware boxes. It's a hoodoo cargo—this is."

Tom came out and stirred the fire and spread his hands before it. "No, I don't reckon there are any skates," he said. "But it can't be long now until somebody comes for the freight."

"I've quit guessing," muttered Van, as he tugged at a heavy case beneath several bales and boxes.

Suddenly the pile overturned with a crash, and a crate of scythe blades broke open, scattering a dozen blades on the ground. Van stooped, picked up one of them, and stood for a moment studying the long sharp edge and its blunt back.

"Say, Tom!" he cried. "I'm going to make a pair of skates out of this scythe blade!" And he took it to the tent.

He gathered a file, a hammer, and a cold chisel, and with the aid of the fire cut the blade into proper lengths. Then he dulled the sharp edges, punched two holes in each piece, and drove them into two pieces of dry cottonwood two inches thick, fastening them in place by driving nails into the wood so that they would intersect the holes in the steel. With the file he squared the blunt edges; and the bits of scythe blade were skate runners.

But it was after noon before Van succeeded in fastening them to his boots.

Then, with bread and meat and a file in his pockets, he hobbled to the river, aided by Tom, and set off up the stream.

"They're fine!" he called as he skated away.

Tom watched him turn the bend above camp. Then he went back and put a camp-kettle of beans over the fire.

Van, keeping near to the river bank, sped on toward Fort Benton. Mile upon mile through the wilderness of bad-land stretches and cottonwood groves he kept his course, the bite of the winter air stinging his face as bend after bend in the crooked stream he rounded in the teeth of the wind. No sound came to him save the szzt—szzt of his skates. Once, far ahead, he saw a pack of wolves crossing the river; and twice he saw deer and antelope near the frozen stream; but there was no camp of wood-hawks or other human beings to be seen.

His spirits were high. He was a splendid skater and a man of exceptional strength and endurance. As he flew past, his eyes swept every grove, but his anxiety waned as each was left behind.

The sun was low and the breeze was stiffening when he came to a long stretch of treeless bottom-land. He crossed the river to avail himself of the shelter of the opposite bank, which was higher, for the wind here was strong. Having gained the other side, he was relieved of the wind's pressure and increased his speed. He now saw, far beyond, a heavy grove of cottonwoods on a high-cut bank where the stream made a sharp turn. In a little time he had reached it and rounded the bend. The wind was strong at his back. It was a welcome help, for the bend was long.

But suddenly he smelled smoke—the smoke of a cottonwood fire. It could mean but one thing. Almost as soon as his nose had warned him, he saw the tops of a dozen lodges among the trees above him. His heart bounded with fear. Bending low, he sought to pass them unnoticed in the shadow of the bank.

But a dog howled in the Indian camp. Then he heard the hoofbeats of a pony and looked over his shoulder. A rider was going for the pony band. There was a scurrying in the camp, and the voices of men were mingled with the wolfish howl of dogs.

They would chase and kill him. Faster and faster his skates met the ice. Swifter and swifter he flew over the river's surface with both fear and the wind lending strength and speed to his strokes. He was nearly to another bend when he again looked behind. They were coming!—fifty or more, their ponies racing over the frozen ground to cut him off at the bend.

He must beat them. Perhaps the river would turn to his advantage if only he could gain the next stretch ahead of the Indians. Straining every muscle in his body, he rounded the bend. The wind was nearly dead ahead now. It almost smothered him in its strength. But it was a race for life, and with his heart pounding loudly he bent lower and struggled grimly toward the next turn. They were coming. They were gaining. If only he could make the bend before they did, he might have a chance. A rifle-ball cut the ice in front of him and went whining away into the bank. Then another splintered the glare ice behind him and he felt the spatter of ice on his hot neck. He was straining every nerve. His temples throbbed with the pressure of blood, and perspiration dripped from his face.

A wild yell sent a thrill through him. He had rounded the bend—made it, ahead of the wild riders. But even as he sensed his victory, his heart sank, for the bend was in the Indians' favor. They were yet nowhere in sight. Madly he raced for the next turn in the river—made it; and there they were. Fifty Indians on the ice before him.

Desperately he tried to stop, ran into the bank, and fell, his head striking the ice violently. A streak of flame and a cracking sound came to him, and then he knew nothing.

Softly the moccasined feet sped toward him. An old warrior with an ugly scar on his wrinkled face squatted near the prostrate white man's feet and murmured. As the rest pressed closer, the old fellow turned his face toward the curious group, his puzzled expression heightened by the sunken lids of a sightless eye. There were soft-spoken words among the others, heavy with wonder. The old man gingerly touched the runners of the skates. "Tst—tst—tst. Ahn-n-n-n!" he said, covering his thin-lipped mouth with the palm of his hand. Others squatted beside him, and one by one they applied their fingers to the skates and murmured.

At last Van opened his eyes. The group fell back, leaving the old man and Van in the centre of a circle. The white man's eyelids fluttered a moment and then closed. The old fellow bent over him with a serious look. Again Van opened his eyes, and, at last conscious of his situation, tried to regain his feet, but staggered and fell. Then he sat up and saw the circle of painted faces about him.

The old warrior with the scarred face motioned to the others and they moved back, forming an immense circle on the ice. Van got to his feet. And then the old man began to slide his moccasins over the ice in imitation of the skater's strokes, at the same time warning him not to try to break through the circle.

Van understood and began to skate for their amusement. He backed and twisted, whirled and jumped, and cut figure eights and pigeonwings. The Indians were amazed. As new groups arrived, the old fellow as master of ceremonies would induce Van to sit down while, squatting at the performer's feet, each newcomer touched the skate runners with his fingers.

"Tst-tst-tst. Ahn-n-n-n!" came from behind the palms that covered their mouths.

Then, satisfied, the old fellow would bid Van skate again.

A hundred Indians had gathered and with rifles in the hollow of their arms stood watching his antics. Fatigue was weakening him. His mind was tortured with thoughts of his fate. And Tom, alone in the camp at Cow Island—what would become of him?

Suddenly, at a wave of the old man's hand, the circle parted up the stream.

"Ho!" cried he of the scarred face. And Van was free.